MW01133707

One Summer of Surrender

(SEASONS BOOK 3)

By

USA Today Bestseller
Jess Michaels

ONE SUMMER OF SURRENDER
Seasons Book 3

ISBN-13: 978-1539559320
ISBN-10: 1539559327

For more information, contact Jess Michaels
www.AuthorJessMichaels.com

To contact the author:
Email: Jess@AuthorJessMichaels.com
Twitter www.twitter.com/JessMichaelsbks
Facebook: www.facebook.com/JessMichaelsBks

Jess Michaels raffles a gift certificate EVERY month to members of her newsletter, so sign up on her website: www.AuthorJessMichaels.com

DEDICATION

For all of you who wanted Stenfax's story. I hope you fall even more in love with him (and Elise).

And for Michael, as we embark on our newest adventure.

PROLOGUE

Summer 1808

Lucien Danford, eleventh Earl of Stenfax, pounded his fist against the door of the London home of one of his best friends. The world was spinning as he awaited a response and he leaned against the barrier as he tried not to cast up his accounts. When the door opened, he staggered through and nearly deposited himself on the foyer floor.

"Where's Folly?" he barked, flinching at the horrified expression of his friend's butler. "And where's my brother? I know they're both here."

The older man swallowed as he caught Stenfax's elbow and kept him from hitting the marble floor. "Mr. Danford and Lord Folworth are in the billiard room, my lord."

Stenfax shrugged off his supportive arm and began to stagger away. "I'll find my own way. Thank you, Ritman."

"Richards, sir," the butler sighed, though he didn't follow.

As Stenfax swayed his way down the hall, the door to the billiard room opened and both his brother, Grayson Danford, and their best friend, the Marquess of Folworth, stepped out. They stared at him, eyes wide with surprise at his state. He knew what they saw. Ruin. Loss. *Pain.*

"Jesus, Lucien," Gray said, lunging for him as he lost his footing.

He fell squarely into Gray's arms and leaned there for a

I

moment, squeezing his eyes shut as he tried not to cry. Or vomit. Or both.

"He's bloody drunk," Folly said, grabbing Stenfax's arm. Together the men led him into the billiard room. "Get him inside, I'll call for coffee."

They placed him on a settee and then Folly rushed out. Stenfax stared up into his brother's face, which was lined with concern.

"She wrote me a letter," he said, an answer to the question Gray had not yet asked.

"Who?" Gray asked softly.

"Elise. Elise wrote me a letter ending our engagement," he said, and the pain of those words hit him with full power. He could hardly catch his breath as he watched his brother's face twist in horror.

"No," Gray murmured. "No! That cannot be possible."

"But it is," Stenfax said, his voice shaking. "She did it."

"Did you quarrel?" Gray asked, still confused.

"No. On the contrary…" Stenfax swallowed as he thought of a night less than a week ago. Then it had been pure pleasure between them. Now it was pure, unadulterated agony. "We were closer than ever."

"Then why?" Gray pressed. "I don't understand. You're to marry in less than a month."

"Not anymore. She's marrying Kirkford. Her letter said she preferred a rich duke to a penniless earl."

Now the horror faded from Gray's face and it hardened with anger. "She said that?"

Stenfax nodded slowly. "In black and white, written in her own hand. So I went to her house and they wouldn't let me in. They said she wasn't home. She wouldn't even fucking see me."

Gray bent his head. "Oh God, Lucien. No wonder you're drunk."

Stenfax reached into his jacket pocket and drew out the letter. He handed it over, not caring that Gray would see the water streaks where angry tears, tears of disbelief, had fallen as he read over and over again the words of the woman he loved.

Gray took the letter and stood up. "Look, let me explain to Folly. Lay here a moment, will you? Just take a few deep breaths, I'll be back and we'll...we'll get through this together."

Stenfax said nothing as his brother pushed to his feet and left the room. Gray's words hung in the air.

Get through this.

There was no *getting through this*. Stenfax had loved Elise for five years. Hell, probably longer than that. He couldn't remember a time when she hadn't been in his life, his younger sister's best friend, trailing after him and his friends and his brother, tormenting him and tantalizing him.

He loved her. And she had told him she loved him. She'd *shown* him she loved him. He squeezed his eyes shut as he tried not to think once again of a night not so long ago when he'd been allowed the liberties only a husband should have.

But he hadn't felt wrong about it. After all, he would be a husband in a few short weeks. But now that night was poisoned. Because everything Elise had ever said or done or claimed to feel turned out to be a lie.

He got to his feet and paced the room, his stomach roiling. He didn't want to be sick on Folly's very nice rug, so he exited the room through the terrace doors. The warm summer air hit him in the face and he shut his eyes as he moved to the edge of the parapet.

The terrace was high above the stone walkway to the garden below. So far down that if a man fell, he would likely die. Stenfax stared at the dizzying distance as the pain in his heart swelled and grew and took over every part of him. Drink hadn't helped. It only made it worse. In that moment, he knew *nothing* could make it better.

He placed both hands on the stone edge of the terrace and pushed up, pulling himself onto his hands and knees on the ledge. He rose to his full height as he widened his legs to stay steady.

He could jump. He could jump from here and there would

be no more pain. No more empty future. No more anything at all.

"Stenfax!"

Lucien looked over his shoulder to see Gray, Folly and Folly's new wife, Marina, standing at the terrace door. All three had horrified looks on their faces, but none more than Gray. Lucien's younger brother had his hands lifted, pleading as he edged toward him.

"What are you doing, Lucien?" Gray asked.

Lucien shrugged as he looked once more at the ground so far below. "I don't know yet," he muttered, hearing the slur in his voice. He was so damned drunk. Would he do this sober?

"Please don't do this," Gray said, his voice catching. "Come down."

Stenfax hesitated. "She left me in a letter. We've known each other since I was thirteen and she left me in a *letter*."

Gray stepped even closer. "I know. I cannot begin to imagine what she's thinking. It was an unforgivably cruel act by a woman who is clearly not what we thought all these years. But she does not deserve the satisfaction of you doing this, Lucien. Nor does our family deserve the devastation that would be caused if you jumped from that ledge."

Stenfax looked over his shoulder at his brother. Gray was shaking all over and his face was so pale it looked like there was no blood left in it.

"How can I go on without her?"

"Please come down," Gray whispered. "We'll talk about it."

Stenfax shifted again, sliding the toe of his boot along the edge of the rock wall. And for the next hour they went on like that, Gray pleading, Folly pleading, Marina pleading and Stenfax uncertain, unsure.

But as the time passed, so did the alcohol fade from his system. The pain increased as the liquor dissipated and yet he still didn't jump.

"Perhaps I'm not man enough to do it," he said at last.

"You're man enough not to," Gray insisted. "Because you know what it would do to our mother, to our sister. To me. *Look* at me, Lucien."

Lucien did so, mostly because his brother's voice got so sharp and so shrill at his order. Gray's eyes were welled with tears and he lifted a shaking hand.

"Please don't do this to me," Gray whispered. "Don't leave me."

Stenfax bent his head. The idea of living without Elise cut him to the core of his being. But Gray's plea hit home. Slowly he reached out his hand and let Gray help him down from the ledge. As soon as he was down, Gray cocked his hand back and punched Lucien square in the face. The physical pain of the punch ripped through him, and for a blissful moment it replaced the other pain.

Folly and Marina both gasped and leapt toward them, but Stenfax grabbed his brother and hugged him. Gray sobbed into his shoulder, holding on to him so tightly that Stenfax knew he would have bruises on his arms tomorrow, as well as a black eye.

But it didn't matter. *None* of it mattered anymore.

"Come inside," Folly said, motioning to the billiard room. "Come inside and we can talk about this rationally."

Gray released him at last and allowed him to shake Folly's hand and accept a quick hug from Marina.

"I'll go inside. I'll do whatever you'd like me to do, after what I just put you through. But let me make one thing clear: I will *never* discuss *that* woman again," he said, lifting his chin and hardening his tone and his heart.

Marina's lips parted. "Dearest, do you think that's best? This is devastating to you and we're here to help you."

He shook his head. "If you want to help me, then do as I just said. We will *never* talk of this night or that woman ever again. And in return I swear I will never do something so rash again."

He didn't wait for the response, but walked back into the billiard room. They followed, their concern as obvious as their heavy stares on his back.

But Lucien didn't care. He had nearly died for surrendering to his emotions. And he knew now that the only way to never let that happen again would be to never let his emotions rule. Not when it came to Elise.

Not when it came to anything.

CHAPTER ONE

Summer 1811

"I'm going home," Stenfax said, not looking at his sister Felicity, nor at Gray and his wife Rosalinde, but continuing to stare into the spinning, laughing, all-too-loud crowd.

Felicity turned to him, her bright eyes filled with worry. God, *everyone* always looked at him with worry these days. It was exhausting. "Oh, please don't go, Lucien," she said, grabbing his hand with both of hers. "We haven't danced an allemande yet."

Lucien arched a brow. "You *despise* the allemande, Felicity. Do try to make your little lies to keep me here more believable."

Felicity rolled her eyes and then stuck just the tip of her tongue out at him. "It was the first thing that came to mind, damn it. But I truly don't want you to go. It's been so long since we all went to a party together and really spent time with each other."

"Yes," Gray said, tilting his head to catch Stenfax's eye. "Stay. I would say the thing about the allemande, but Felicity already got caught in that lie, so give me a moment and I'll come up with an excuse."

"No excuses," Rosalinde said gently. "We only wish to enjoy your company, as Felicity says."

Stenfax sighed. "You are almost impossible to refuse when you band together to work against me." He shook his head. "*Almost.* Look, I'm not enjoying myself, this party is far too crowded and that orchestra is quite possibly the worst one I've ever heard. My head is throbbing and in a moment I may start bellowing about politics and ruin the entire night. It's best for me to just go now before the evening deteriorates into fisticuffs with some seventy-year-old who never wants change to happen in his lifetime or anyone else's."

Gray sighed and exchanged a glance with the women before he clapped a hand on Stenfax's shoulder. "Very well, it seems there is no dissuading you. At least allow me to walk you out."

Stenfax nodded before he bussed Felicity's cheek, then Rosalinde's, and said his goodnights. The two men then walked through the ballroom and out into the much quieter foyer. Stenfax caught a footman's eye and lifted his hand to send the boy scurrying for his horse. It would likely take a few moments to arrange it with his leaving so early.

"What is it?" Gray asked when they were alone in the small space.

Stenfax let his eyes fall closed. This was a topic he did not broach. Not with anyone. "Nothing," he said softly.

Gray turned to face him head on. "You are shutting down, Lucien. Locking us out. It's like…" Stenfax looked at his brother in time to see Gray's face twisted momentarily. "It's like before."

Stenfax flinched at his younger brother's raw expression. The pain of it forced him to think of that night three long years ago when he'd nearly ended his life. There had been ripples of that horrible experience through every moment of his existence since then. Changes that could not be denied. Hearing the faint whisper of fear in his overly protective brother's voice was one of them.

He placed a hand on Gray's forearm and gently squeezed. "It's not, I assure you."

There was a moment when Gray's relief was plain, but then it was gone. He tilted his head slightly. "I don't mean to be crass, but how long has it been?"

"Been?" Stenfax repeated, though he was utterly aware to

what his brother referred.

Gray folded his arms. "You know. Since you had a woman."

Stenfax looked out the open door into the darkness. He shook his head. "I don't know. A long time."

That was a lie, of course. He knew exactly how long it had been since he'd last been with a woman. Over a year. And even then, the sex had been a rote act meant to release some tension. It never really worked.

"Go find some pleasure," Gray suggested, dragging Lucien back to the present. "Wake yourself up. Burn off some energy."

"I don't know," Lucien said with a sigh.

"Let me know for you," Gray insisted. "Please. I don't want to see you shrivel into yourself ever again."

Stenfax heard Gray's true worry and he clenched his fists at his sides. "Very well," he said, more to appease his brother than for his own pleasure. "I'll go to Vivien Manning's."

Gray's eyebrows lifted. "The Mistress Matchmaker? Actually, that's a wonderful idea. Get a mistress, someone to see more permanently."

Stenfax shook his head. "No, I'm not in the market. I-I don't *think* I'm in the market. It's just that I've always gotten on with Vivien and she can help with someone discreet. Maybe I'll want her for a few days or even a few weeks. Perhaps you're right that it will help."

"Good." Gray said the words, but as Stenfax looked at him he could still see his brother's deep concern.

He frowned. "It's not about *her*," he said, addressing at last the subject that always hung unspoken between them.

Gray bit back a humorless laugh. "It's *always* about her."

Stenfax's shoulders rolled forward in defeat and he sighed. "Yes, I know."

"Here you are, sir!" the footman called out as he came up to the door outside with Stenfax's mount.

"Goodnight," Gray said, mercifully releasing Stenfax from the requirement of addressing the subject further.

"Goodnight," Stenfax returned, tipping his head to his brother before he walked out and swung up on his mount. He rode the animal out into the street and turned him toward Vivien Manning's, where there was always a party in full swing.

But even as he vowed to do exactly as his brother suggested, he knew it wouldn't help. It never did.

The Duchess of Kirkford sat in a quiet side room in the home of the notorious Vivien Manning, her hands folded in her lap and her mind reeling. She had come here by appointment and had been led through what could only be described as an erotic bacchanalia. She had seen things she'd never even imagined before, from women performing wild dances in very little clothing to couples having sex right in the main room to the intense scrutiny of the audience.

She shifted in her chair at the thought of it, and the tingling awareness those thoughts created. She was in over her head, it seemed.

The door to the room opened and a woman swept through. As Elise got to her feet, she gasped. Vivien Manning was younger than she'd imagined during their brief correspondence, and far more beautiful, with a coil of blonde hair piled high on her head and a serene face.

"Your Grace," Miss Manning said as she extended a hand.

Elise shook it in a fog and then stammered, "O-oh, please, call me Elise. I don't want to think about being the Duchess of Kirkford when I'm here."

Vivien lifted a brow at that declaration and then motioned Elise back to her chair. She took the one opposite and suddenly blue eyes were sweeping over her, taking her in, judging her. Elise swallowed hard at the other woman's perusal. Would she live up to whatever standard she was being compared to?

"Elise," Miss Manning finally said. "Then you must be

certain to call me Vivien. And I'm happy for that familiarity, but there *is* one issue."

Elise's stomach turned. "And what is that?"

"I may call you by whatever name you ask for, my dear, but the material point still exists that you *are* the Duchess of Kirkford."

Elise squeezed her eyes shut for a moment. "Yes," she said softly.

"It isn't that I haven't matched the occasional titled widow," Vivien continued. "But never one of such a high rank. So I must ask, what is it that brings you to my door? Pleasure or something else?"

Elise stared at her. The concept that a woman would come to Vivien for a pleasure match had never occurred to her. She shook her head. "I—must I say it?"

Vivien nodded. "You must. I need to know the circumstances I'm involving myself and others in if I am to continue. But this place is known for its utter discretion. So you needn't worry that your story will become fodder for others."

Heat was burning Elise's cheeks now and she could hardly find the words as her head spun. At last she drew a long breath and said, "I am in a tenuous position. My husband died in November of last year. There was a drawn out struggle between two cousins to determine who would be his successor."

"Oh yes, that was very public."

"*Very* public," Elise said with a shudder as she thought of the cruel and violent pair who had battled so fiercely for the prize of the title. "Neither was the best choice, but the one who won the title in the end is a bastard of the highest order. He and my late husband had that in common, it seems. And it has been determined that I have been left nothing."

"Nothing?"

Elise lifted her hands to rub her arms, as if she could make the cold go away when it generated from icy terror about her future. "No. I have been allowed to stay in a smaller home in London thus far, but that 'kindness' is threatened to soon come to an end. Whatever money I saved from my pin amount is all I will be settled with and it is a pittance, Vivien. I have no family left—my parents died two years ago—and nowhere else to go."

"You *could* reenter Society and find a new husband," Vivien suggested gently.

Elise shook her head. "The mourning period requires I wait an additional three months before I even *think* of reentering Society. If I returned now looking for a husband, I would be shunned. And my husband's death was in a duel over a married woman. I think you probably know that."

Vivien inclined her head once and Elise stammered, "Th-then you know that scandal will likely make any attempt to marry well even more difficult. It's a nearly impossible path, but to be someone's mistress..."

She trailed off, and Vivien said, "It seems the one of least resistance. And it will allow you to retain some autonomy that a marriage would not."

"Yes," Elise whispered.

"I understand," Vivien said, leaning forward. "But you may not. Now I must ask you some rather indelicate questions. Did you like sex?"

Elise jolted at the very direct and unexpected question. But Vivien held her gaze steadily and it didn't seem that this was a way to make her uncomfortable. She just wanted to know.

"I—once," Elise admitted, her mind going to one glorious night that felt like a lifetime ago. Hands on her, a mouth on her, eyes that were filled with love that seemed to pierce to her very soul. She shook it off and jumped to her feet, pacing away before she added, "But I also know a great deal about enduring."

Vivien stood and faced her. "Most men do not want a mistress who *endures*. Or at least looks like she is."

Elise swallowed hard. "Well, I suppose it would be nice if I..."

She broke off, and for the first time Vivien smiled gently at her. "If you liked the man?" she finished for her.

Elise nodded slowly. It was hard for her to imagine that

could be so. It was hard to think how she wouldn't compare any man who offered to protect her to the one she had been married to…or worse, to the other man she'd loved. The one she tried so hard not to think about.

But maybe it *was* possible.

"I'll do my best, Elise," Vivien said, moving toward her. "Now, why don't you go out into the party? Grow accustomed to the…the public displays. Just your appearance here will generate some interest and I will think on the prospects available and see what I can do to help you."

Elise almost sagged with relief, even as sheer terror gripped her stomach. She forced a smile. "Thank you, Vivien. I appreciate it more than you could possibly understand."

Vivien nodded. "I've asked one of my guards to watch you. No one will bother you. And if I find someone tonight, I'll have you meet with him in a private room. Not to consummate a bargain, of course. But to get to know him. Will that suffice?"

Elise let out a broken sigh. "Yes."

Vivien motioned her toward the door. She followed the silent instruction and exited into the hall and walked toward the main room. This was not the future she had pictured for herself so many years ago.

But this was where she was. And she would have to come to grips with it and do the best she could.

Stenfax stepped into Vivien's closed off foyer and approached the guard at a table in the vestibule. The man looked up. "Good evening, sir. Your name?"

"The Earl of Stenfax," he said, tossing his card on the table.

The man picked it up, examined it a moment and then began to flip through a long list before him. He glanced up. "I'm sorry, sir, you don't seem to retain a membership in Miss Manning's club. Would it be under another name for anonymity?"

Stenfax pursed his lips. "No. I'm not a member. I haven't been here in a long time, actually, but Miss Manning and I are acquainted."

The man looked him up and down, sizing him up, looked at his card again and then nodded. "I see. Well, wait here, will you? I'll have someone check."

Stenfax nodded as the man scurried off, card in hand, to talk to another guard at the entrance to the main house. The second man left as the first retook his position at the door. Stenfax paced off rather than taking a seat in the vestibule, looking over the painting that hung in the foyer. He shook his head with a chuckle.

Vivien was still Vivien. The painting had been done by one of the most popular portrait painters of the day, but this painting was of a naked lady, legs spread lewdly as a man knelt before her, almost in prayer. Stenfax wanted to feel something as he looked at it, but there was nothing that stirred in him.

Nothing but vague memories that he pushed away with internal violence.

"Stenfax."

He turned at his name and found Vivien, herself, had come out to greet him. She was a beautiful woman, with a lush body and thick blonde hair. She also wore a swooping neckline that left very little to the imagination. And still he felt nothing.

This was going to be an embarrassing waste of time, it seemed, but he stepped forward. "Vivien," he said, taking her hand and placing a kiss against her knuckles. "You look lovely."

"Thank you," she said, and motioned him to follow her into the hall. They walked the length, past rooms where moans echoed and halls where Vivien's pleasure parties were in full swing. She took him to her small office in the back, and when he entered he stopped dead.

There was a scent in the air. One that felt...*familiar*. Jasmine and earth, sweet and sultry. All at once, his cock stirred and he swallowed hard as she closed the door behind him.

"I'm surprised to see you here. You haven't been to my club

in over a year," Vivien said, gliding a hand toward the liquor at her sideboard.

He shook his head. "Yes, well, I was to marry, if you recall. I steered away from such things. But when my engagement to Celia Fitzgilbert dissolved, I just..."

"You had no heart for it?" Vivien offered.

He shrugged. "Something like that. But I've been told that taking a lover might improve my mood around others. So I came here in the hopes you might help me find discrete companionship for a very limited engagement."

Vivien tilted her head and a sudden knowing smile crossed her lips. "You came here *tonight*. Of all nights."

He wrinkled his brow, not understanding her tone. "Yes," he said slowly.

"Looking for a temporary lover," she continued.

He nodded. "Yes. Is there something I'm missing?"

Vivien shook her head, but that secret smile remained tilting her lips. "Not at all. I think we understand each other perfectly. *She* is looking for a longer term agreement, you know."

Stenfax blinked in blank misunderstanding. She? Vivien must be referring to the larger "she". To all the women who came to her, seeking to be matched with a protector.

"I'm certain that is true. That is what you do, after all. But you must make it clear that I am not in that market. At least not at this point. I don't want to mislead anyone."

Vivien nodded slowly. "I will make it clear, Stenfax, I assure you. This might even make it easier."

Stenfax stared at her. She truly did have the oddest expression on her face, but before he could question her more fully about odd behavior, she motioned him toward the door. "I'll take you to a room and bring you what you desire."

Stenfax sighed and drew in another whiff of the rapidly fading scent in the room. It stirred him as nothing else in his presence that night had. Then he followed Vivien down the hall, through winding corridors where more moans and cries floated from various rooms. She stopped at one and motioned him in.

"Here is where you will meet with the lady. Talk, and if you can come to an agreement, do as you will. I hope I'll see you after for a drink." She bobbed her head as he entered, and left.

Stenfax slowly looked around the room. There was a bed in the corner, draped in rich red satin. A fire burned in the enormous fireplace and a black velvet settee was set before it. This was one of Vivien's finer rooms, he thought. And not, it seemed, one where other guests could spy. He verified that with a quick sweep of the room for hidden looking holes.

Satisfied, he shrugged out of his jacket and draped it over a chair near the bed. There was a window beside it and he moved to it. He could see the terrace off the ballroom to the side and there were couples milling about on it, kissing, touching, one was even making love. His body thrummed and he shut his eyes, thinking of soft hands on his flesh, warm lips covering his, thinking of...

Elise.

His eyes flew open and he shook his head to clear the image. No, he would *not* think of Elise tonight. She would not pollute a night of pleasure with a willing stranger.

As if on cue, he heard the door behind him open, and the rustle of skirts before the door was shut. He slowly turned, a smile of welcome on his face for the lady who would bring him that pleasure.

But when he saw her, the smile fell. The blood drained from his face, his hands began to shake. He stared at the woman who had entered the room and his mind began to scream at him.

Elise. It was Elise. She was standing there at the door, staring at him with an expression of shock and horror that had to match his own.

And she was *gorgeous*. He hadn't seen her in three long years, a circumstance organized and planned impeccably because looking at her would be too painful. And it was, for everything about her was even more beautiful than he remembered.

She was a statuesque beauty, a good head taller than most

of the women in their set. This meant she towered over many of the men, but never him. She had always fit perfectly in his arms. But it wasn't just her height that gave her presence.

Elise was stunning. She had an intelligence to her face and coupled with her high cheekbones, her full lips, her bright green eyes and her light red hair, she had always been the kind of woman men turned to look at as she passed.

He thought all that in the fraction of the second as he saw her standing there, and then his brain lurched, recognizing not only that she was there, but where *there* was. Elise was at Vivien Manning's, a house of ill repute, where men came to have their pleasure and women came to find protection.

She was here in a room with him. Anger rose in him, betrayal and confusion mixing to a toxic level. He swallowed hard and found his voice.

"What the fuck are you doing here?"

CHAPTER TWO

Elise's heart was racing so fast that it felt like she would collapse. She stared across the room and couldn't believe what she was seeing. This was a dream she'd had so many times that she wished she could pinch herself now to prove it wasn't real.

Only she knew it was. Lucien was here. Just a few feet away from her. And he was so utterly beautiful. He was tall, impossibly tall, with thick, dark brown hair and eyes the color of rich molasses. He had a strong jaw and full lips that she had pictured moving over hers a thousand times in the three years since she'd seen or touched him last.

"Answer me," he snapped, his hard, harsh, broken tone shattering the spell between them. "What the hell are you doing here?"

As he asked the question a second time, he started across the room toward her in long, certain strides. He looked like a bull racing across a paddock at an intruder, and she should have been afraid. But she wasn't. Not even a little. She stood her ground without effort and sucked in a long whiff of his scent as he crowded into her space and all but pinned her to the door behind her.

"What do you *think* I'm doing here?" she managed to ask, pleased she could talk at all, let alone sound as cool and detached as she somehow did.

His jaw tightened, the muscle along it twitching, and she had a powerful urge to lean up and kiss him there, feel him move beneath her lips. But she didn't do something so foolhardy.

"*Why?*" he finally shouted.

Before Elise could answer, the door behind them flew open and Vivien raced in, a guard behind her.

"What is going on in here?" she cried.

Lucien glared at Elise one last time, then pushed past her toward Vivien. "I could ask you the same bloody damned thing, Vivien."

Elise remained facing away from them, but flinched at his anger and his familiarity with Vivien. He was here, after all, and he had obviously been looking for someone to take. Not her, of course, not her. But someone.

"Isn't this what you wanted?" Vivien asked.

Elise spun around to see his face when he answered her. It twisted in pure horror. "Is that what *she* told you?"

Elise gasped. "No!" she burst out. "I had no idea it was you I was being led to meet."

Vivien nodded. "I didn't tell her a thing, nor did she ask for you. But I assumed...I assumed..."

"What?" Lucien fumed, raising his hands in animated fury. "Why in God's name would you assume I wanted *this*?"

Vivien lifted both eyebrows. "You showed up here after over a year, on the very night your former fiancée did. I assumed you were hoping to match with her. The coincidence—"

"Is just a coincidence," Lucien snapped.

Rejection stung every part of her, but Elise lifted her chin as he turned to look at her at last. His dark gaze flitted over her and his pupils dilated.

"Get out," he growled

Elise wrinkled her brow. "Are you speaking to me?"

He shook his head very slowly. "Not you. Vivien—get out."

Vivien folded her arms and let out a bark of laughter. At her side, her guard stirred, but she held up a hand to still him. "I beg your pardon?"

"Get out," Lucien repeated, this time softly, almost gently.

"I shall not," Vivien said. "I don't trust you won't...well, you're very angry, Stenfax."

Elise stared at him. He was, indeed, very angry. It all but pulsed through his every fiber. But she still wasn't afraid. Not in the slightest. Nor did she want to escape that anger. She deserved it, after all. What she had done to him deserved anger and revenge and a great deal else. She had already served part of her penance in a desperately unhappy marriage.

Perhaps this was the rest.

"It's all right," Elise said, casting a quick side glance at Vivien. "You may leave us."

Vivien looked between her and Stenfax. She flitted her hand and the guard stepped from the room, though Vivien remained. "Are you certain?"

The answer to that question was no, but Elise nodded regardless. "Yes."

Vivien shot another look at Stenfax, then inclined her head and backed from the room, drawing the door shut behind her.

Lucien was silent for what felt like a lifetime. His nostrils were flaring and his hands were fisted at his sides. "I would *never* lay a hand on you in violence, *ever*."

She nodded slowly, thinking of his history. Even if she didn't know what his sister and her former best friend Felicity had endured in her marriage, she knew him well enough to trust what he said was true.

"I know," she whispered.

He swallowed. "You're here for a man."

Heat flooded her cheeks, but Elise forced herself to nod again. "I-I am."

His face twisted yet again, but this time it wasn't a mask of anger, but of pain. He just as quickly flattened that into bored disapproval. "Why?"

Stenfax couldn't stop looking at Elise. Smelling her, that same jasmine scent he'd caught in Vivien's office earlier. The one that had set his body on edge. It was hers. Of course, it had always been hers, he'd just allowed himself to forget. Forced himself to forget.

Now it all but filled him up and he wanted to rip the gown off her body and bury himself in her. Cover himself in that smell and in her taste and her feel.

How he hated them both for that lingering want.

He turned away and walked across the room, back to the window where he'd first seen her. "Answer me," he said.

She cleared her throat and he faced her. God, but she was calm. Cool. He so wanted her to *react*, but of course it was only him who was affected. Just as it had always been.

"Why do you think?" she asked, repeating her earlier answer. It was just as unsatisfying now as it had been then.

He clenched his hands at his sides. "Damn it. It's a straight question, give me a straight answer."

She shrugged and broke eye contact with him at last, looking instead toward the fire across the room. "*He* left me with nothing."

He. Of course she meant her husband, the Duke of Kirkford. The man she had left him for, thrown him over for, all those years ago. The mention of him sent a shockwave of fresh pain through Lucien's body. Fresher than he'd allowed himself to believe when he'd spent so much time ignoring it and denying it.

"Do you want me to feel *sorry* for you?" he spat out, his voice as hard as diamonds.

She slowly returned her gaze to him. "No. I would never expect that. You asked me a question and those are the facts."

He drew in a few deep breaths. "And so because he left you destitute, you are turning to…to…"

He couldn't even say it.

She nodded. "I'm looking for a protector."

He paced away, his blood boiling even hotter at her simple answer and her calm demeanor as she gave it.

"You're a duchess." He strode over to the fire and pressed

21

a fist against the mantel. "A lady."

"Many ladies do the same, either because they are forced by circumstance or because they wish an affiliation. And that is why I turned to Vivien. She is said to be good at providing discreet help in such matters."

He spun on her, glaring at her. "Oh, well, as long as it is *discreet*, Your Grace."

Her eyes suddenly lit up with a flash of anger and he was torn back in time to a girl with red braids. He had tugged them and she had spun on him with the same rage on her face and given him a set-down. He had dreamed of her for the first time that night, boyish dreams where he stole a kiss.

He forced himself back to the present as Elise took a long step toward him, her hands gripped at her sides and her shoulders shaking. "*You* are here, aren't you? I assume you were looking for a tumble. So don't you dare judge me, Lucien."

She had said his name. It was the first time he'd heard it from her lips in three long years and it washed over him and turned him inside out. He found himself moving on her again, one step, two, three, and her eyes widened, and yet she didn't move, just as she hadn't the first time he did this a few moments before.

He crowded into her space and tried to tell himself he was making an attempt to frighten some sense in to her. It was a lie and he didn't care. He didn't care about anything except the fact that he was so close to her he could feel the warmth of her skin pulsing out, reaching for him.

He lifted his hands and closed them around her upper arms. The first time he'd touched her in so long. She caught her breath and slowly her gaze moved his hands. His did the same and they stared together at his big, darker fingers around her pale, soft skin.

Need coursed through him, more powerful than anger or hate or anything else he had ever felt. And he couldn't deny it. He couldn't deny her and her power over him even after everything she'd done, everything she'd broken.

He leaned in and pressed his mouth to hers. He expected her to remain cold, or even to turn away, but instead she made a muffled little cry in the back of her throat and opened her lips.

And he was lost. He drove his tongue into her wet heat and stroked hers as he yanked her closer, into his arms, molding her body to his. She pulled her arms loose from his grip and wrapped them around his neck, whimpering as she lifted against him like she could find a way to get closer even though they were flattened together in an embrace.

He tilted his head, making his kiss deeper and tasting sherry on her tongue, probably to help her with her courage in coming here. He tasted sweetness that was only Elise and had only ever been Elise. He hadn't realized how much he missed that taste and now he drowned in it, losing all ability to control the kiss or himself.

She didn't seem to care. She thrust her tongue against his in equal desperation and need, sucking him in, meeting him halfway, her body grinding against his with longing that matched his own.

He staggered backward, keeping her in his arms as he fell into a seated position on the black velvet settee. She straddled his lap, her gown tangling around her legs as she dug her fingers into his hair and pressed herself hard against him.

He wasn't going to stop this. That thought ripped through his mind, tearing past all the high emotion. This was going to happen, right here in Vivien's parlor, on a night when he'd come looking for a woman so he would forget the very one writhing on his lap.

This was so much better.

He kept kissing her even as he gripped a hand at the hem of her skirt and began to bunch it, shoving it up the length of her long legs and revealing pretty stitched stockings. He stroked his fingers over the satiny smoothness and knew that his arousal was probably eminently obvious to her. His cock was pressing against her thigh and it wasn't subtle.

She broke the kiss at last and stared down at him, green eyes

23

wide and slightly off focus. "Is this real?" she whispered as he let his hand span the side of her thigh.

"I hope so," he growled. "But do you want it?"

She nodded immediately. "More than anything."

There was nothing else to say. As she shifted to accommodate him, he shoved her skirt up and around her hips and gasped. She was utterly bare from the waist down, save for those stockings. He lifted his gaze and her cheeks brightened with color as she turned her face away.

Of course she would wear nothing beneath her gown. She was here to seduce a lover. And she was, though not the one she had likely thought she would end up with.

He shoved aside the brutal jealousy at that thought and let his hand brush over her hip, then down and around to stroke over her sex. She sucked in a breath through her teeth and shut her eyes as he trailed his fingers over her entrance. She was wet already. Slick with need, and his cock actually twitched as he stretched her open slightly and found her clitoris. He pressed a thumb to her and she jolted with a soft cry.

He leaned up, finding the soft column of her graceful neck, and began to kiss there as he stroked her, stroked her, teasing her pleasure from her until she was jerking against him with a wild rhythm. She was on the edge now, ready for release, and that's when he pulled away.

Her eyes fluttered open and she glanced down at him with wild, wide eyes. Eyes that dilated when he moved his hand to the flap of his trousers and opened them, releasing his hard cock into the space between them.

She licked her lips and he nearly spent right then and there. He took a few long breaths as she locked eyes with him. Slowly she reached out and wrapped her fingers around him. He gripped his own fingers into the settee cushion as she stroked over him once, twice, three times. Then she shifted up on her knees and positioned herself over him.

He felt her heat and then her slickness wrapped around him. He slid into her one inch after another as both of them let out a long, shuddering sigh. As he filled her completely, he realized this was like coming back to a home he'd thought he'd lost.

He didn't want to feel that way, but there it was, and he stared up into Elise's beautiful face, taut with pleasure and tension, and he knew in his heart that he had been waiting for her, waiting for *this*, for three long years. Now he was here, and he lifted his hips up into her as she shuddered in pleasure.

She rocked against him, meeting his driving rhythm as she ground down over him hard and steady. He cupped her hips, moving her against him as he lifted his mouth to her throat again.

As she took him, Elise began to make soft moans. Her rocking motion grew erratic and her face twisted with pleasure. She was close to release and he lifted his fingers up to cup the back of her head and tilt her face toward his. She opened her eyes and met his stare, her hair falling around them as her mouth contorted and she let out a shaky cry of release. Her body tightened around his, milking him, drawing his own pleasure to mix with hers. He lifted her aside and grunted as he spent away from her and then collapsed back on the settee, his breath coming hard and his heart pounding not just with release, but relief.

But as that same heart rate slowed and the ability to have rational thought returned, he let his gaze slide back to Elise, who was curled up next to him on the settee, her hair tangled around her face, her dress still hitched around her hips.

Need, want, relief aside, Stenfax realized what he had just done. The thing he'd vowed never to do again. He'd just let Elise have the upper hand over him. He'd just revealed a piece of himself to her.

And *that* was an utter mistake.

CHAPTER THREE

One a warm summer night very much like this one three years before, Elise had stood before this man and given herself to him. Not since that night had she felt such passion and desire and utter pleasure. Certainly not with her husband, who she had never found or even sought pleasure with. Not even with her own hand, when she feverishly tried to reach the same heights she recalled with Lucien.

Now her body thrummed with pleasure and peace, like this was where she had been meant to be all along. And in truth, it was. What she had done, how she had turned away from Lucien, it never should have happened. *This* was where she belonged. He was where she belonged.

She smiled up at him and he met her gaze cautiously. When she saw the hardness of his expression, the anger and the hate still bubbling below the surface, her peaceful feeling faded into numbness. In that moment, she saw nothing had truly changed between them. And why would it? Lucien didn't understand what she'd done, he never would.

Even if she could explain it to him, he'd never forgive her. Trying to find those words seemed futile, they would only cause more pain for them both.

For him, this night hadn't been about reunion or repair, but something else. As if to prove it, he shoved to his feet and began to fix himself. He turned to the chair and caught up his jacket, flinging it over his shoulders without looking at her.

"*That* was a mistake." His tone was so harsh that it felt like a physical strike.

She closed her eyes and drew in a few long breaths so her own voice would be calm when she said, "I see."

He froze in his motions as she got to her feet and let her gown fall back over her half-naked body. She reached down and began gathering up the pins that had fallen from her hair and then moved to a mirror across the room to fix it. She could almost see the tracks of his fingers through her locks, and God, how she wished she could keep them there as proof that he had wanted her.

"You shouldn't do this," he said softly, his tone much gentler than it had been.

She looked at him through the reflection in the mirror rather than facing him. That was too hard in this moment, she didn't want to give him too much. She already had.

"I understand that you feel that way," she said.

His eyes narrowed. "But you'll do it regardless"

She nodded once. "I will. You don't have a right to tell me what to do, Lucien. Not anymore."

His jaw stiffened at those words and he straightened even taller. "No," he growled. "I suppose I don't. Good luck, Elise."

She flinched. That was the first time he'd said her name in what felt like forever, and it was said with such anger.

"Goodbye," she whispered.

He shook his head as he strode to the door and closed it none too gently behind him. When he was gone, she bent forward, gasping for breath as she gripped the table before her.

For years he had avoided seeing her. She knew that was true. She'd heard all about the lengths he went to in order to do just that. She'd never fought it, never tried to subvert him, because she knew in her heart that seeing him was going to be too painful.

Tonight, she realized she was right. It *was* too painful. She had never stopped loving Lucien, not for one moment. She loved him still, even though all his love for her was long gone, destroyed by a choice he thought she'd made. A choice she *had* made that was worse than anything else she'd ever done in her entire life.

She straightened and looked at herself in the mirror. She could almost see his fingerprints on her skin, almost still feel his breath against her body, his mouth on her mouth. Those sensations would fade, of course, and she would miss them as desperately as she missed him.

"But that is the past," she said to her reflection, wishing her voice didn't tremble. "He is gone and all your wishing doesn't change a thing. You can't let this steer you from your course. It is still the only way."

Saying the words out loud to herself helped, at least a little, and she finished fixing her hair before she threw her shoulders back and walked from the room. She didn't dare take a look back at the settee for fear she would burst into tears. She just walked out with as much pride as she could and made her way back into Vivien's main hall.

In the hours that had passed since she arrived here, much of the debauchery had ended. There were still couples or groups here and there, drunkenly playing. But most of the couples had either gone to rooms to finish their pleasure or gone home after completing it.

Stenfax was nowhere to be found. Elise sighed, uncertain if she were happy or sad about that fact. She didn't have to decide, luckily. Her thoughts were interrupted when one of Vivien's guards approached her.

"Miss Vivien would like to see you before you depart, Your Grace."

Elise swallowed. Of course Vivien would. The scene she and Stenfax had created tonight would warrant such a request. She wouldn't be surprised if Vivien would not help her anymore because of it.

And then all would truly be lost. But perhaps that was what she deserved, after all.

She followed the man back to the office where she'd first met with Vivien and found the woman sitting at the large desk.

When she rose, Elise was surprised to find that Vivien was no longer dressed in her provocative clothing, but in a plain, pretty gown with a modest neckline. She rose as Elise stepped inside.

"Would you like tea or brandy?" Vivien asked, motioning to both on the sideboard.

"I'm not certain which will calm me more," Elise admitted.

Vivien's smile was gentle. "Brandy then."

She poured it, and she and Elise took the same seats by the fire where they had begun hours before, though it now seemed like days.

"I am sorry about the misunderstanding earlier," Vivien said when Elise had taken a sip of the brandy and focused on its burn down her throat.

Elise shrugged. "I suppose it *was* a wild coincidence that Lucien would show up here the night I did. Does he come often?"

"Once he did, but he hasn't for a long while. He used to show up here to ask for—" Vivien cut herself off. "Well, it doesn't matter. I understand his tastes a bit better now after seeing you. Why he was so particular back when he came regularly."

Elise wrinkled her brow, for she didn't understand what Vivien was going on about. She certainly didn't want to hear about Lucien's conquests. The very idea made her stomach hurt.

"Will you refuse to help me now?" she asked.

Vivien's eyes widened. "You are direct."

"I'm too exhausted now to be anything but," Elise admitted.

Vivien sat back in her seat, and once again Elise knew she was being judged by the courtesan. "I know the story, of course—*everyone* knows the story about you two. But I feel like the story isn't exactly accurate. So help me understand what it is between you and Stenfax before I answer your question."

Elise set her glass down. "There is nothing between us," she whispered, trying not to think of the passion of their joining such a short time before. "He hates me, that's all that's left now."

"Hmmm," Vivien murmured. "*Hate* isn't what I saw."

29

Elise pursed her lips. Vivien's words gave her hope and hope was far too dangerous to dare have now. She dropped her gaze. "You are wrong. I threw him over three years ago. As you said, you know that. Everyone knows that. He *hates* me for it, that is the only thing I know for certain."

Vivien was silent for what felt like an eternity, and then she said, "You threw him over for a higher title and more money."

Elise slowly nodded. "Yes."

"And it isn't more complicated than that?"

Elise jerked her face up and found Vivien watching her very intently. In three years no one had ever asked Elise that question. No one had ever doubted her decision had been based on anything more than simply wanting to be a duchess rather than a countess. Rich rather than financially compromised. No one had ever searched for the truth in the lies she'd been forced to tell.

But the truth was too dangerous to share.

"No," Elise lied.

"And after tonight, after this thing with Stenfax, do you still *want* a protector?"

That question was utterly loaded. Before Stenfax came into the room, Elise had been trying to find a way to make her choice sufferable. She'd been telling herself she might come to like whatever man took her to his bed. That this would be all right.

Now that dream was dashed. No one would ever be Stenfax. No one would ever come close.

"I must," she said, her voice cracking. "Nothing changed tonight."

Vivien arched a brow, her incredulous look telling Elise that she didn't believe her. Elise didn't believe herself, so she couldn't blame the observant courtesan. Still, Vivien didn't argue with her or press for more. She just nodded.

"I told you I'd help you and I shall," Vivien said. "Give me a few days and then come back. I'll have a few gentlemen for you to meet and talk to. Perhaps one of them will catch your eye."

Relief cascaded over Elise, tempering some of her harder emotion. Slowly she rose to her feet. "Thank you, Vivien. I appreciate your help."

Vivien murmured her response and walked Elise to the foyer and her waiting carriage. But as Elise got inside the vehicle and was taken back to her home, she knew the things she'd said to Vivien were all lies.

Everything had changed tonight. And yet she could expect nothing from Lucien. She would just have to live with these new memories and place them alongside all the others. It was all she *could* do.

Lucien paced his bedroom, still smelling Elise on his clothing, his skin, his very soul. He was still utterly confused by what had transpired between them tonight.

Seeing her had sparked feelings he'd promised himself he had quashed forever. Touching her...well, that brought out something different entirely.

He knew exactly why Vivien had thought he wanted to meet with Elise. It was because when he'd come to her club in the past, he had always asked for women who looked like his former fiancée. Trying to purge himself of her by taking women who reminded him of her had never worked.

Taking *her* hadn't worked either. Instead of cleansing his system of her at last, he now throbbed with renewed desire for her.

Certainly it would help to talk to someone about this subject, but who could he turn to? Gray and Felicity would both react poorly if they knew what he'd done. Felicity had once considered Elise her best friend. When Elise had left him, it had been as much a betrayal of Felicity as himself. And Gray had watched him nearly kill himself over Elise. He had even intervened in Stenfax's engagement with Celia because he feared what his emotions on this very subject would do.

In short, both his siblings hated Elise. *He* hated Elise.

Except it hadn't felt like hate when he saw her, when he touched her, when he buried himself deep inside of her.

Nor had he felt hate when he saw the flicker of pain in Elise's eyes when he turned away from her after their joining ended.

No, that feeling had been guilt.

He slammed a hand down on the table near him and growled out, "Shit."

There was no reason for him to feel guilt over what he'd done. Elise had come to Vivien's seeking a lover and she'd said she wanted him. She'd *proven* she wanted him. If he walked away from her at the end, wasn't that exactly what she'd done to him all those years ago?

Didn't that make them even in some way?

He pursed his lips at the vengeful thought. Whatever he believed of Elise, she was still a lady. And he had used her in the worst way possible. Yes, he had thought of her pleasure, but that didn't mean he hadn't used her. It wasn't gentlemanly, to say the least.

And when he was honest with himself about his cruelty, he also had to be honest with himself about the need to address it. Only that meant seeing her. Going to the home she lived in now, the dower house, and *seeing* her. Tomorrow would be best, to clear the air on this matter immediately.

A thousand thoughts went through his head. Was he just doing this to look at her again? No, no, of course not. That was pure poppycock.

He was going in order to set things straight between them. He was going so that he could walk away from her and no longer be haunted.

At least he hoped he wouldn't be haunted. Right now that was *all* he felt.

CHAPTER FOUR

Lucien swung down from his horse and looked up at the modest townhouse that rose before him. Elise's dowager residence, the one she had taken up after the death of her duke. It had been a long time since he'd approached her door. The last time was when he'd come demanding to see her after she wrote her letter dismissing him.

Pain shot through him and he tamped it down with violent force. This wasn't even the same house. That horrible night he'd gone to her father's residence. There was nothing remotely similar about the experiences.

He strode to the door, extending a card to the butler who greeted him. He thought he saw the barest reaction of surprise when the man read his name, but he didn't turn Lucien back. Instead, he led him to a parlor off the foyer and went to ascertain if Her Grace was in residence.

Lucien pinched the bridge of his nose as he paced the room. What if she refused him again as she had that long-ago night? His jaw tightened at the thought that she would do such a thing...*twice.*

The door behind him closed and he turned toward the sound to find Elise standing there. He caught his breath. At Vivien's club she had been dressed in vibrant colors and a plunging neckline. Today she was wrapped in mourning black and covered modestly. Her hair was pulled back in a simple chignon rather than the glorious waves he had pulled down to cover them as they made love. She also had a slight darkness beneath her eyes, the only mar on her skin telling the tale that their night together had affected her the same way it affected him.

She was beautiful. Almost unbelievably beautiful.

"Wh-what are you doing here, Lucien?" she whispered.

He swallowed hard, trying to remember the answer to that very good question. It was near impossible when his mind was whispering how easy to would be to cross the room and kiss her. Better yet, unwrap her from those bloody mourning clothes and have her right then and there.

"I came to talk to you about last night," he burst out, too loudly, he knew.

Her lips thinned as she pressed them together and her expression grew cool and distant. "I don't think there's anything more to be said, my lord. You made yourself very clear."

He cleared his throat. This was not going exactly the way he'd planned it as he tossed and turned in his bed the night before. He drew a long breath and started again.

"It was ungentlemanly...the way I acted last night. From start to finish." He met her gaze and forced himself to hold it. "I'm sorry."

There was no mistaking the shock on her face at his apology. Her eyes went wide as saucers and her lips parted. But she swiftly wiped the reaction away, returning to the cool and collected Elise he wished so desperately to move. Beneath that stony exterior had to be the Elise he'd once known. That woman *had* to exist. Didn't she?

"You needn't be," she said. She shifted slightly, the only indication of her discomfort. "I—we were both swept away, my lord. I'm as much to blame for what transpired in Vivien's club as you are."

He took a long step toward her. "Why did you, Elise? Why did you let me?"

The coolness fled again and her face crumpled ever so slightly. She seemed to be fighting a battle within herself, truth versus lies, vulnerability versus the walls she'd erected between them for some unknown reason.

"Because——" she began, her voice trembling.

But she didn't get to finish. Before she could, the parlor door flew open and the new Duke of Kirkford strode inside.

Elise flinched as her late husband's pompous cousin marched into her parlor unannounced and uninvited. Of course, that was what he always did, declaring that the dower house was his property as much as any other he had inherited.

And the way he often looked at her, Elise wondered if he felt he had some right of claim on *her*, as well. The new duke's focused attention was part of the reason she was so desperate to escape these walls.

She moved to face him and shuddered. It wasn't that he was physically ugly. Like his late cousin before him, Ambrose, the ninth Duke of Kirkford, had an interesting face that likely many a woman would desire. But he was, also like his late cousin, unbearably stupid, oafish and rude.

Ambrose let his gaze flit over her from head to toe in the same way he always had and likely always would. Elise felt stripped by the action and she swallowed back the rise of bile in her throat.

Then he turned his attention to Stenfax and a sneer turned up his lip. "What the hell is *he* doing here?"

Elise caught her breath as Stenfax took yet another step toward her. His face was stony now, but the slight twitch of his lip told her that he was getting very angry. She would have to manage this carefully or else she might end up with a dog fight in her parlor.

"Your Grace, I believe you know the Earl of Stenfax," she said, trying desperately to make this a normal meeting in a normal parlor between two normal men. "My lord, my husband's cousin, the new Duke of Kirkford."

"We know each other," Ambrose said, his tone heavy with

disgust. "And *you* haven't answered my question, Elise. What the hell is he doing here?"

Stenfax's hands fisted at his sides. "Her Grace has every right to keep company in her own home, I believe."

"*My* home," Ambrose corrected. "Which I allow her to reside in because of my good graces."

Stenfax barked out a humorless laugh. "Your good graces are fully on display, I see."

Ambrose's brow wrinkled and it took him a moment to understand the jab. Elise marked the exact moment it became clear, for he scowled. "My cousin hasn't even been dead a year and you're here sniffing after his wife. She threw you over, man—how hard is it to get it through your skull?"

Stenfax stiffened and Elise stepped into the space between the men, reaching back to press a hand to Stenfax's chest in the hopes it might keep him from lunging. She felt his heart rate increase when she touched him and ignored how her own did the same.

"Lord Stenfax is an old friend of my family," she said softly. "He made a social call and I appreciated it. But he was just leaving."

As she said the last, she turned slightly toward Lucien, sending him a look she hoped he would understand and accept. Once upon a time, he had been able to read her expressions. It seemed he still could, for his lips pressed even harder together and he shot her a look that could have frozen the Thames even in the depths of summer.

"I suppose we have concluded our business," he said. "Good day, Your Grace."

The hardness of his tone was like a knife to her heart. A moment before Ambrose interrupted, Lucien had seemed to soften a fraction. And he had tempted her with that softness to almost reveal the truth to him. To almost confess how she loved him and had never stopped loving him.

What a foolish act that would have been. She supposed she owed Ambrose a thank you.

"Good day, my lord," she whispered as Stenfax strode from the room without so much as a goodbye for Ambrose.

Once he was gone, Ambrose let out a low chuckle. "He always was a lap dog for you."

Elise let out her own humorless laugh. "I don't think many would dare describe the Earl of Stenfax as anyone's lap dog, Ambrose."

He walked away from her, going to the sideboard to pour himself tea without taking her leave or even offering her a cup. "I'm going to ask you again, Elise. Why was he here?"

She clenched her hands behind her back. "It's bad enough you just stride into my home whenever it pleases you. Can I not have *any* privacy in my meetings?"

"You can once you're gone," he said, arching a brow as he made his point. "With your *inheritance*, I'm certain you can afford a hovel of some kind. And you're pretty enough to trade on your body to eat, I'm sure."

She flinched at his plain talk, a reminder of where she stood in the world at present.

"You should have more gratitude, Elise." He drew out the word *gratitude* as he set his cup down and moved toward her. "I'm a kind man to allow you to stay here when I could easily place you on your arse in the street."

She swallowed hard. "Very kind, yes."

"Are you certain you don't have a way to repay my kindness?" he asked, reaching out a finger to trace the line of her arm.

Even though the heavy fabric of her mourning gown, Elise felt the pressure of his touch, and she shut her eyes and tried to keep calm. "Only with my words of thanks, Ambrose."

He rolled his eyes and went back to her sideboard to shove a cake into his mouth. He didn't finish chewing before he said, "I could think of better things to do with those lips. One day you'll realize your position, Elise, and you'll come around to my way of thinking on the subject."

She lifted her chin. "I don't think so," she hissed.

37

He swallowed his food as his eyes narrowed on her. "On such a high horse, are you, you frigid bitch? Makes me wonder how my cousin caught you when you clearly hated him as much as you hate me."

Elise pressed her lips together to remain silent on the subject.

He tilted his head. "You think I don't know he had secrets? And he knew how to use them to get what he wanted. If I knew yours, *Your Grace*, would you open your legs to me, too?"

It was almost impossible to retain her calm when he was dancing on the dangerous edge of the truth.

"I don't know what you're talking about," she said, forcing her shaking hands behind her back once more. "But all this excitement has given me a headache. Perhaps you could call another time, Ambrose. With some advance warning."

He glared at her, then shrugged. "Fine. But we're not done, *Your Grace*. Not by far. I'm going to sniff out all of those lies you've been telling. So you'd best ready yourself. Everything that was his is mine now. *Everything*."

He turned and left the room and Elise sank into a chair, gasping for breath. God, how Ambrose reminded her of her husband. Toby had often given her that same look. One of disgust and distain. Living with him, being his prize in a cruel game, his decoration and his toy, had been hell.

She would not put herself in the same position ever again. A mistress had more freedom. If matched correctly, a mistress had power and autonomy. That was why she'd made these choices. And she couldn't stop now.

In fact, she had to work harder. She had to escape this house. And she couldn't allow Lucien's reappearance in her life to steer her from that course. No matter what feelings he stirred in her.

Stenfax paced Gray's parlor, his hands clenching and unclenching at his sides. He'd been meant to meet his brother today at this very hour and hadn't been able to escape the duty. But after what he'd just experienced at Elise's home, he wished he could.

Gray was going to see. He was going to know the truth. And that was going to open a Pandora's Box of trouble.

As if on cue, Gray entered the room and Stenfax stopped pacing a moment to greet him. Before he could, Gray leaned back and shut the door. "What is it?"

Stenfax squeezed his eyes shut. Damn Gray for knowing him so well. When he looked at his brother again, he fought for some level of control over his emotions.

"Nothing. We were supposed to meet and here I am. Where is Rosalinde?"

Gray pressed his lips together. "Out with Felicity, and *you* are changing the subject. What is it that makes you look so…so…*angry?*"

"What's wrong with being angry?" Stenfax ground out. "Can't a man be frustrated by his horse throwing a shoe or it raining when he wanted it to be fair or the state of the damn roads?"

Gray leaned back. "But you aren't angry about a horse and it's not raining and the roads between your home and mine are perfectly fine. But if you don't want to talk to me, by all means, stew in your own rage. Just don't do anything that you can't take back."

Stenfax flinched. The night he had perched himself on a terrace over Elise and nearly taken his own life had changed him. But he knew for a fact it had also changed Gray. His brother was sometimes desperate to protect him. Desperate to help.

He let out his breath in a long sigh. Maybe he needed help. Maybe he needed the harsh counsel Gray would provide if the truth came to the surface. A cold splash of reality.

"What do you know about the new Duke of Kirkford?"

As he had expected, all the color slowly drained from

Gray's face and he stared at Stenfax in wordless horror for a few long beats.

"You didn't."

The disapproval and horror in his brother's tone made Stenfax turn away. *This* was what he'd sworn to Gray and Felicity that he wouldn't do again. This was what he'd promised himself he wouldn't do ever since the day he heard Elise's husband was dead.

And yet here he was.

"Don't judge me," he said softly.

"I bloody well will judge you," Gray barked, stalking over to the sideboard and splashing scotch into a glass. He downed it in one slug and poured another that he handed over to Stenfax. "It seems you have no judgment of your own, so I must have it for both of us. You went to Elise?"

Stenfax shook his head. Gray was not just his brother, he was his best friend. And right now, he needed that, even if Gray would snort and condemn his way through any explanation.

"I didn't go to her. Not at first," he said slowly. "In fact, I did what you suggested and went to Vivien's. She was...there."

Gray's mouth dropped open. "I'm sorry. Elise...as in the Duchess of Kirkford Elise...was at Vivien Manning's?"

Stenfax nodded. "It seems she was settled poorly and is considering finding a protector to get her out of her financial state."

"And she went to you," Gray said, folding his arms. "After what she did."

"No, we were placed in a room together. Elise didn't orchestrate it. I am almost certain she didn't." He caught his breath as he heard how ridiculous that sounded. "It doesn't matter. We ended up in the same room and I...I couldn't help myself, Gray. Have you seen her in the time since we parted?"

Gray drew in a long breath, obviously trying to calm himself down. "No. I avoided it just as you did. I think we all did."

"Well, she is...she's more beautiful than ever," Stenfax

admitted softly, images of her spinning up in his mind. "She's just the same as she was three years ago, and yet she's even better. I knew it was wrong, but I touched her and then...then it spiraled out of control."

Gray's eyes went wide. "I see. So you made love to her."

"Took her is a more apt description," Stenfax said, his tone grim as he thought once more of his ungentlemanly actions. "I know I shouldn't have. But it was magnificent. And yet how could I? How could I do such a thing?"

"You judge yourself but not her?" Gray asked.

Stenfax shrugged. "My actions are the only ones within my control, so they are all I choose to judge. I should have walked away the moment she came into the room. But I didn't. So I...I went to her home on Tinley Square this morning."

Gray threw up his hands. "Lucien!" he burst out. "Goddamn, it is bad enough you did something so foolish at Vivien's, but to follow Elise across town?"

"I know, I know," Stenfax said, waving off his brother's sharp disapproval. "I just couldn't stop myself. I needed to apologize for my behavior. But the new duke came in, interrupted us. It's Kirkford's cousin—Ambrose, I think his name was."

"Yes, I heard he won the battle for the crown," Gray said. "Buffoon that he is."

"Well, he is a buffoon with power. And he seems to be wielding it over Elise. So I want to know more about him." He finished the sentence and heard it ring in the air around him. He heard the desperation to his tone, the protectiveness that should not have been reserved for Elise after all she'd done.

And even if he hadn't heard it, he certainly saw all those things reflected in Gray's expression. His brother moved toward him, catching his arms and staring up into his eyes.

"Listen to yourself," Gray said softly, almost gently. "Damn it, Stenfax, listen to your words and remember the past. If you aren't capable of doing so, then listen to me. Elise pretended to be something she wasn't. She pretended to care not just about you, but about *all* of our family. She wound her way into our lives and our hearts, none more than you. But she was false, Lucien. The moment she was offered a higher title and a larger purse, she turned away from you, from all of us."

"I know," Stenfax said, fighting the urge to defend Elise from his brother's accusations. After all, they were true.

"You know, but you don't seem to recall the consequences of her actions." Gray backed away. "I saw what it did to you, I saw what it did to Felicity. Elise's betrayal came so quickly after Felicity was widowed, after she escaped that bastard she married. She needed Elise and it broke her heart nearly as much as it broke yours. I watched what that woman did to you both. And she didn't give a damn about your feelings."

Lucien shook his head. "Yes, I realize everything you're saying is true. And I understand exactly why you and Felicity despise Elise. Why you wouldn't want to see me ensnared in her trap once again."

Gray stared at him for what felt like forever. "You understand, but you still want to know more about the new Duke of Kirkford."

Stenfax pressed his lips together. "Yes," he whispered at last.

Gray sighed, shoving a hand through his hair as he paced away to the fire. He stared at the dancing flames for a moment before he turned back. "Marina and Folly are back in Town. She is related to Kirkford, third cousins or something to the effect. We could ask them."

Stenfax nodded slowly. "Yes. I'm certain she would know something about the man. Arrange the meeting if you would. I'm certain the two of them would love the chance to go through all my mistakes on this subject just as you have."

Gray gritted his teeth. "It's not a matter of going through the mistakes, Lucien, it's fearing the costs if you forget the past. Don't forget, we were all there that night. We all know what we almost lost thanks to *her*."

Lucien bent his head. "I understand."

Gray moved toward him, wrapping an arm around him. "It's out of love that I worry," he reminded him. "And it is out of love that I ask that you don't see her again, Stenfax. Please."

Stenfax sighed heavily. Then he nodded. "I won't."

He felt his brother relax with that vow and Gray stepped away. But as Gray changed the subject of their conversation to far less explosive topics, Stenfax couldn't help but feel guilty. The fact was, he had just lied. He had every intention of keeping a close eye on Elise.

He just hoped he'd be able to control himself while he did it.

CHAPTER FIVE

Elise sat at a corner table in Vivien's club, suitors surrounding her. She forced a smile at one of the men who was talking to her, even as her mind wandered.

In truth, this process was not that different from the courtships she saw in Society. Of course, the setting was vastly different, with couples openly displaying and often openly relieving their lust. And the men were more obvious with their intentions and desires when they spoke to her.

But otherwise, they circled her, chatting with her mindlessly, peacocking around her with displays of how they would take care of her financially or physically.

She let out a long breath as her closest companion leaned in. It was the Viscount Highbridge who showed her the most attention and demanded the most from her in return. She observed him a bit more closely.

He was older than she was by at least twenty years. She thought that at one point he might have been a friend of her late father's, for she felt as though they'd met a long time ago. That didn't seem to dissuade him. He kept leaning toward her. Kept letting his hand rest on hers as they spoke.

There was no doubting his interest, but also no denying that she felt nothing at all when he looked at her or touched her. Not even a flutter of interest.

Damn Lucien. He had thrown her entire plan on its head by...by...well, by being him and reminding her how much she wanted him. One little taste of him and the flavor of all else was utterly ruined.

"Would you care to dance, Your Grace?" Highbridge asked, sending meaningful looks to the other men circling her.

She forced her attention fully on her companion. "That would be very nice, thank you."

She rose and the rest stood with her, murmuring their desire for her to save another for them, as well. She nodded as she took Highbridge's arm and let him take her to the dancefloor.

When he did, her eyes widened. Unlike at a Society gathering, the dancing here was far more scandalous. Couples pressed close together, moving in sensual displays. Some kissed and touched openly.

She let her gaze flit to Highbridge. "I, er..."

He shook his head. "We are only getting to know each other, my dear. I have no expectation that we will engage in such behavior." He took her hand and spun her onto the floor. "Yet."

She caught her breath at the idea of doing such things with this man—ever. It was one thing to give oneself as a mistress, quite another to grind against a man in public without heed for those around her.

Could she do that? Or was she just entirely over her head?

"You look very lovely," Highbridge said, his gaze sweeping over her in appreciation.

She blushed. She was wearing another of her old gowns, altered so the neckline was scandalously low. She still didn't feel comfortable with the air on so much of her skin. But at least it wasn't black. How she hated black, and she still had a few months left of wearing it.

"Thank you, my lord," she said, forcing a small smile for him.

He returned it with a wider version. "What are you looking for in a protector?"

She swallowed. No one had asked her that question before. She thought on it a moment, then said, "Someone who would allow me independence."

He arched a brow and his chuckle grated along her spine.

45

"Independence. Well, most mistresses have a great deal of that, depending on the man. Are you saying independence in that you'd like independence to bring other men to your bed or independence in that you want your own home and funds?"

Her lips parted. Another man in her bed? Great Lord, she was nervous enough about one.

"The second, my lord," she gasped out.

"And what are you willing to *do*"—he tugged her closer suddenly, his hand straying far too low on her back—"for your independence?"

She drew a breath to calm herself and said, "My lord, I—"

He turned her as she spoke and suddenly they spun directly into the very tall, very red-faced figure of Lucien. Lord Highbridge released her immediately and she staggered at the sudden sensation of being free.

"Stenfax," Highbridge said. "Didn't know you were here tonight."

He shot an uneasy look in Elise's direction and she blushed. Damn it, Lucien would ruin everything. He *was* ruining everything, standing in the middle of the dancefloor, glowering at the man who had held her. Didn't he know everyone would talk? In this room they would whisper, but this juicy bit of gossip might also filter wider into Society.

"I came to dance with Her Grace," Stenfax said slowly, calmly despite his tense expression. "May I cut in?"

It was said as a question, but there was no mistaking it was an order. Highbridge knew it, as well, and turned toward Elise. "I hope we'll speak again soon, Your Grace."

She inclined her head with an apologetic expression. He backed away, and when he was gone, Stenfax grabbed her hand and spun her into the steps of the dance. He glared down at her, wordless.

She huffed out a breath. "What are you doing, Lucien?"

His anger felt like a pulse between them as he growled, "Highbridge is a bastard."

She shook her head. "Yes, I had that sense, myself. But that isn't really your concern, is it?"

The hand on her back tightened, drawing her closer. He leaned down and his face was dangerously close to hers. "Isn't it?"

"No," she whispered. "You've made that clear. So you don't get a say."

She could see how frustrated that response made him, though she still didn't know why. He clearly despised her, she had earned his ire. What more was there to say? Except he kept coming to her. He kept inserting himself in her life like he had some desire to be there.

And it was unfair. And wonderful. And too hard to express.

The music ended, but Lucien didn't release her. They stood in the middle of the dancefloor, staring at each other. And slowly, Elise became aware of something else. Almost everyone in their vicinity was staring at them. Mistresses, straying ladies, gentlemen of industry and titled ones...they were all watching them.

"Lucien," she whispered.

He nodded slowly. "I see them."

He backed away from her and issued a smart bow. Then he caught her arm and guided her from the floor. The others began to go back to their business, and she expected him to simply deposit her outside the ring of the dancefloor and leave, abandoning her to the consequences of his touch and his anger yet again.

But he didn't. Instead, he marched her through the ballroom, out the door and down a long hall. He threw open the first door he came to and all but dragged her inside. She stared around her. It was a billiard room, with almost nothing inside but a few chairs and a large table for the game.

He leaned back and locked the chamber door before he moved on her. "I thought you weren't coming back here."

She folded her arms. "I never promised that. What happened between us changes nothing."

"No, your ambitions never had any relationship to me," he

snapped, his eyes flashing.

She caught her breath at his cruel accusation. To him it was true. To her...

"Or do you want to clarify anything about the past?" he asked.

She flinched. For the first time, he was directly offering her a chance to explain herself. But what good would it do? The truth would only hurt him as much as the lie had. More, probably. And it wouldn't change what they'd lost. What she'd done.

"If you hate me so much, if you blame me so much for our past, why the hell do you keep seeking me out?" she asked. "And publicly? Do you know what might come of that little scene in the ballroom? People will talk."

He shook his head. "Vivien is strict in her policies. No one talks about what they do here."

She pursed her lips. "I can't imagine you are truly that naïve. Perhaps they won't say *where* they saw us, perhaps they'll never admit to the most humiliating parts. But someone *will* whisper to someone else that they believe you and I are circling each other again. It's too good a piece of gossip not to repeat."

She could see that statement hit home, for he scowled deeper. And oh, how she wished she could cross the room and kiss that frown away the way she'd been free to do so long ago. She wished she could make him touch her because he loved her, not as some surrender to physical need despite his negative feelings toward her.

How she wished so many things.

"Honestly, Stenfax," she whispered. "I don't understand you at all."

"Don't you?" he said, and he moved on her suddenly, taking three long steps that closed all the distance he had initially placed between them. "It's a funny thing to hear you say that, considering *you're* the one who did the unthinkable."

He was so close, she felt the heat of his body, she smelled the scent of him. He was so close that all she had to do was lift her hand a fraction and suddenly she was touching him. Her fingers curled against his chest and he caught a hard, harsh breath as he stared down at her.

"*This* is the unthinkable," she whispered. "Being with you again was something I never thought would happen again. And it's impossible to be near you and not want...want..."

He cut her off by bending his head and pressing his lips to hers. Once again, there was little gentleness in that action. It was like he had been fighting need and lost, washed away by desire that overcame hate.

It stung, but it didn't change the fact that his lips on hers were the most wonderful thing she'd ever felt. She wrapped her arms around his neck, tilting her head to grant him more access. And he took it, spinning her around to lift her onto the billiard table, pushing her legs open so he could step inside and tug her even closer.

She unbuttoned his jacket and slid her hands inside, reveling in his warmth and the flex of his muscles beneath his shirt. He grunted against her mouth, pushing his hips against hers so that she felt the growing evidence of his desire. The length of him nudged at her and she shivered in anticipation of what was next to come.

Because she had no doubt what that was. She wanted him. He wanted her. And this was an avalanche that couldn't be stopped.

"Undress me," she whispered, drawing her mouth away from his and staring up at him.

He held that gaze for a long moment then slowly nodded. He pulled her to her feet and she turned her back to him. He unhooked her dress slowly, his fingers brushing her skin as he parted the gown bit by bit. He leaned in, his breath hot against her neck, and kissed the flesh he'd revealed. She sucked in a gasp of pleasure at the erotic pleasure of his mouth.

When she was unbuttoned to the waist, he whispered, "You're not wearing a chemise."

She nodded. "The gown is too low in the front. All of them showed."

He was silent for a moment and she looked over her shoulder at him. His expression was one of both excitement and frustration at her answer.

"Right now it's only you and me," she reminded him, hoping that this odd jealousy her decisions seemed to inspire wouldn't keep him from the next moment they could share together.

He nodded slowly and slid his fingers beneath her dress, pushing it forward so it drooped around her elbows. She shoved it the rest of the way off and then turned as she shimmied it over her hips and stood before him, naked.

He swallowed hard, his eyes darting over her from head to toe. It had been a long time since he'd seen her like this. She knew she'd changed in that time and she hoped she wouldn't disappoint him.

He reached out and let just his fingertips graze over her skin. Starting at her collarbone, he feathered his touch over her, then lower to her breast, flicking one naked nipple gently before he cascaded lower to her stomach, over her hip, and his hand fell away before he could cup her sex.

"I often wondered if I dreamed our night together all those years ago," Lucien said, his voice rough. "You couldn't have been so perfect as I imagined. But…you are more perfect. More beautiful."

The compliment was the first gentle thing he'd said to her since his return to her life and Elise caught her breath at the power of it. Her love for him swelled from deep within her, taking over every other thing in the room. Making her want to confess dark secrets, beg for forgiveness for a past she couldn't change.

But if she did that, this beautiful moment would pass. And she needed it, so desperately.

"I want to see you," she whispered, motioning to his clothing. "Will you let me?"

Stenfax hesitated and she frowned. Was he so wary of revealing even his body to her, knowing that she'd taken so little care of his heart in the past? But finally he slipped his jacket off and went to work on his shirt.

When they'd been together a few days before, both had remained mostly clothed. Today she caught her breath as he peeled his shirt away.

He was so remarkably beautiful. He was muscular but not thickly built. No, his was a wiry strength, deceptive but powerful. She stepped toward him without ordering herself to do so. Her hand lifted, shaking as she pressed it to his warm, naked flesh.

He sucked in a breath when she did so and his eyes fluttered shut. She smoothed her palm over him, memorizing the lines of his body. She leaned in and pressed her lips to him next, tasting his warm skin with delicate little licks.

He groaned above her and she lifted her eyes without stopping her kisses. His eyes were open now, staring as she caressed him.

She wanted to bring him pleasure. That fact rocked through her with enormous power. She wanted to give him something without expecting anything in return.

She knew one way to do it. A thing she'd only seen in books and in the naughty paintings that hung on Vivien's walls, had never once considered doing for her late husband. But for Lucien?

Well, for Lucien she would do anything and everything.

She reached down and unfastened his trousers. He pushed them away and his cock came loose. He was already hard as she dropped to her knees on the soft carpet before him. Hard and ready.

She shivered and looked up at him as she cupped him. His eyes were wide, his expression uncertain.

"What are you doing?" he whispered.

She didn't answer him with words, but by guiding his thick cock to her lips and taking just the head of him inside. He let out a sound of pleasure that cracked the silence of the room and his hands came down, fingers tangling in her hair.

She took him deeper, loving the feel of him in her mouth, the taste of him. She wasn't entirely certain what one was meant to do in this situation, so she went by instinct, taking him as deep as she could manage, then withdrawing until he almost exited her lips. She rolled her tongue around his length, she sucked gently. When he moaned, she worked harder, faster, seeking his pleasure without giving a thought to her own.

Not that she didn't feel her own. There was an intense power to this act. An eroticism that made her wet as she took him.

She felt him getting close to the brink. She sensed his crisis and she saw it approaching as she looked up his body to watch his face.

But he didn't allow her to steal his pleasure. With a low cry, he caught her elbows and drew her up his body, forcing her back against the billiard table once more. He balanced her on the edge of it, lifting one of her legs to hook around his back as he thrust deep and hard into her willing body.

She arched at the feel of him entering her in that swift, slick stroke, pleasure exploding in her entire body. He ground his hips against hers as he held her gaze steadily. She wound her arms around his neck and did the same, even as she lifted into his thrusts, rubbing herself against him to increase the pleasure for both of them.

The intensity of their locked stare, combined with his expert thrusts, brought her to the brink swiftly. She moved to turn her face, but he cupped her chin and held her there, making her look at him as her crisis at last hit. She jolted against him, watching how his pupils dilated as she came, feeling how his body quickened as she milked him with her pleasure.

He let out a low, needy moan as he pulled away, turning so she couldn't watch him in his pleasure as he had watched her. It was disappointing. She gave, he never did.

And she knew why. She knew *exactly* how she'd earned his reticence.

He reached down and grabbed for his trousers, shoving

them on without looking at her. She edged herself off the table and found her now-wrinkled gown. Stepping into it, she sighed. It felt like an impossible chasm between them, regardless of how powerful their joinings were.

"Do you need help buttoning it?" he asked.

She turned and found he already had his shirt on. He was tucking it into his trousers, almost back to the man he had been when they entered the room.

"Yes," she said, putting her back to him a second time. If he had taken his time unfastening her, he buttoned her with swift and almost detached efficiency.

She shook her head and faced him when he was done. "You keep doing this," she said. "*We* keep doing it, regardless of everything else."

He had begun tying his cravat and his hands stilled at her observation. He lifted his gaze to her, holding it steady just as he had when he took her. Only now his expression wasn't one of desire and connection. He was wary of her.

He bent his head again, not looking at her as he said, "I want to stay away from you, Elise. I know it's the right thing to do. But I..." His voice dropped. "I can't."

She caught her breath. That was the closest to an admission of caring she would likely ever again get from him. And it opened up possibilities in her mind. If he wanted her, perhaps that could solve her problem on so many levels. Being with him could help her escape Ambrose and his ugliness, but it could also be an opportunity to slowly heal the wounds between her and Stenfax.

After time, she might even be able to explain herself to him and have him understand.

She stepped toward him. "I still need a protector," she whispered.

His head jerked up and he looked at her. She could see he understood where she was going with that statement. Immediately, he shook his head. "That can't be me, Elise."

Pain tore through her at that plain statement. He wanted her, but only because he couldn't fight that feeling. It was a weakness in his eyes, not a future of any kind.

She nodded slowly, forcing her voice to remain neutral as she said, "No, of course not. I see that."

He went back to tying the cravat, though she noticed his hands moved a little more slowly. He looked at her from the corner of his eye. "But you haven't found a protector yet."

"No."

He finished tying the knot and grabbed for his discarded jacket. As he put it on, he said, "If I come to you again, will you turn me away, Elise?"

She swallowed hard. The past two times he'd touched her had proven what she wanted deep inside. And if these moments were all she'd ever have with Lucien, she would be a fool to lie and say she didn't want them.

"I can't," she admitted. "I can't turn you away, Lucien."

His expression softened just a fraction. "Neither can I. Even if I hate myself for it."

She winced at that assessment, and at the way he turned away from her and moved for the door. He unlocked it and turned back toward her.

"Goodnight, Elise."

She nodded and whispered, "Goodnight."

And then he was gone, taking all the air in the room, all the warmth in her body, and a piece of her heart with him.

CHAPTER SIX

Elise stood at the full-length mirror in her chamber, staring at the image that stared back at her. She was dressed in one of her altered gowns, this one a warm pink and recut so low that she feared if she bent the wrong way she'd give everyone a show. Her hair had been done in a loose and sensual way, and she looked every bit the temptation she felt she must be.

Yes, she was ready for a return to Vivien's lair. Yet, just as she had the past few nights since her last encounter with Lucien, she hesitated. She hadn't been back since then. She had dressed, she had been ready, then she'd changed her mind.

Going there just felt so damned hard now.

There was a light knock on her door and then it opened, revealing Elise's maid, Ruth. Elise tried to brighten her countenance as she turned toward her.

"I was thinking that I won't go tonight, Ruth," she said. "I apologize for wasting your time yet again, but I'm still just not feeling well. You can help me out of the dress and then let Madison know that he may put away the carriage."

Ruth pressed her lips together and swallowed hard. For the first time, Elise noticed how flushed the young woman was, how nervous she seemed. "Your Grace, er…the duke is here."

Now the color went out of Elise's own face. She hadn't faced Ambrose in almost a week, not since he made that threat about finding out Toby's long-buried secrets.

"Is he?" she said, working hard to get a handle on her tangled emotions.

Ruth nodded. "He demands to see you right away. And he said to tell you…"

She trailed off, and Elise took a step toward her. "It's all right, Ruth. I understand these are not your words. Tell me what he said."

"He—he said if you weren't down in three minutes, he would come up here and get you, whether you were dressed or not."

Elise sighed. "I assume he'd love to catch me undressed. It seems my time is ticking down. I will go to him. Thank you, Ruth."

The maid bobbed out a nod and left the room. Elise tossed one more look at herself. She was dressed like a harlot and that would likely only serve to entice Ambrose more. She grabbed a shawl and pulled it around her shoulders, trying to cover herself a fraction before she headed out of her chamber and down the stairs to the parlor.

She drew a long breath before she entered, tamping down fear and anxiety at coming face to face with her adversary.

"Your Grace," she said, her tone falsely airy as she entered the room. "I did not expect you tonight."

He turned from the fire and his eyes all but bugged out of his head as he looked at her. She tugged at the shawl but knew it did little good. Ambrose ogled her scandalously exposed body, and the way he shifted let her know he was now aroused.

She thought of the gun she kept in her room upstairs and wished she had found a place to hide it on her person. She didn't trust this man one iota.

"Good evening, Elise," he said, stepping toward her. "Don't you look fetching tonight. Were you going out?"

She swallowed hard. Thus far she'd been able to keep her trips to Vivien's secret. The courtesan had assured her that she would never give a membership to her club to Ambrose, as he was, in Vivien's words, "trouble". Elise certainly had no intention of telling him herself.

"No," she said. "I was just reading and planned to turn in

early."

His eyes lit up and she swallowed past bile. "Excellent. I am going to a ball. An old friend of yours, the Marchioness of Swinton, invited me."

His crowing tone grated along Elise's spine and she couldn't help her flare of temper. "Well, bully for you, Ambrose."

He moved on her a long step, his smile fading. "Watch your tongue. You're coming with me."

Elise stared at him in shock. "No!" she cried out when she could find words. "I most certainly am not. My mourning period is a few more months, Ambrose. I cannot go to a ball while I'm in black."

"I didn't ask you, Elise," he said, snatching a hand out to catch her arm. Her shawl fell away and he stared even more blatantly as he began to drag her across the parlor.

"Stop," she insisted, digging in her heels and tugging back against him. "Stop it this instant."

He yanked her closer, her face now mere inches from hers. "What would you prefer I do, Elise? Stay in with you? Take you to bed?"

She froze in her struggles as she looked up into his face. He looked deathly serious now, like he was hoping she'd fight him.

"No," she whispered.

He smiled. "Then to the party you and I will go."

She squeezed her eyes shut a moment, willing tears not to fall. "Why? *Why* do you want me there, Ambrose?"

He caught her chin in his hand, a mirror of what Stenfax had done when they made love a few days before, only without the gentleness and care Lucien had shown her. Ambrose squeezed, just enough to hurt, not enough to bruise.

"Because I want all of them to know I have the same power as my cousin did. I want *him* to see I have all the same claims."

"Him?" Elise asked, trembling and hating herself for showing that weakness.

"Stenfax," Ambrose clarified. "Your earl is sniffing around

you again and I don't want to encourage that to continue. Now, we are late. So let's go."

He grabbed for her arm again and she tugged a second time. "Please, at least let me change. This gown is utterly inappropriate."

He smiled as he looked her up and down and then began to pull her toward the door again. "No, Elise. It's just perfect."

Stenfax stood in the middle of the Marquess of Swinton's ballroom, party in full swing around him, but he was hardly there at all. His mind kept taking him to Vivien Manning's club. To Elise. To the fact that he'd gone back to the club three nights since he last saw her and not found her there.

It had taken everything in him not to go back to her dower house and confront her. Take her.

He blinked as the swarm of mamas and their eligible daughters who currently surrounded him all spoke seemingly at once, asking him questions and trying to make their charges the one in his sightline.

They were pretty enough ladies, of course. Some were accomplished. All would very likely make a fine countess.

But Stenfax had gone down this road before. Just a year ago, he had become engaged to Rosalinde's sister, Celia. He'd sought out a woman who would never ask for his heart, a woman who he'd never be tempted to give it to.

The engagement had failed spectacularly, though it had given rise not only to Gray's happy marriage to Celia's sister, but to a friendship with Celia that Stenfax very much appreciated.

Still, he had no intention of trying to do that again. Certainly not during this Season of all Seasons, when he was tangled up in lust and confusion over Elise.

He smiled at the crowd around him, placating,

noncommittal. It was funny, as much as he was the center of attention tonight, he had also sensed something else in the crowd when they looked at him. People would occasionally whisper behind their fans and stare.

He had no idea what that was about, but it was utterly tiresome indeed. He wanted to run.

Just as he was about to find a way to do so, his sister Felicity began to make her way through the crowd. "Ladies, might I borrow my brother for a moment?" she asked, her dark blue eyes snaring his in a pointed stare.

He wrinkled his brow. Felicity didn't look very pleased. The women around him made various moans and groans, but she still took his arm regardless and led him away.

Only when they had paced to the edge of the ballroom did he feel as if he could breathe again. He faced Felicity with a smile. "Thank you for coming to my rescue. Was my drowning very obvious to you and Gray and Rosalinde from across the room?"

Felicity's expression tightened. "I was not coming to save you," she said, her voice strained. "I have heard...troubling things."

Stenfax's body went on guard because her expression was so dark and pointed. This did not seem a subject that should be discussed in the middle of an eavesdropping ballroom, so he caught her arm and guided her from the crowd, out into the hall and down to a parlor away from prying eyes and straining ears.

As he shut the door, he faced her. "What sorts of troubling things, Felicity? Is someone speaking unkindly about you?"

Her face lost all its color. "What would someone have to say about me, Stenfax?"

He shook his head. "I have no idea—certainly there is not a blemish on your character. But you seem so upset, I had to wager a guess that you had been hurt by someone."

"This isn't about me," Felicity hissed, turning away from him. "Damn it, Lucien, I have heard you and Elise are...*entangled* again."

He froze in his spot, staring at his sister's pained expression. "Who said that?"

She caught her breath. "You do not deny it first, but ask the source?"

He clenched his teeth, thinking of Elise's admonishment at Vivien's a few nights before. She said then that word of his barbaric, possessive display could possibly spread outside the club and into the ballroom. Now it seemed she was correct.

"Who?" he repeated.

Felicity folded her arms. "It was on the wind. And...and Gray verified it when we were speaking a few moments ago."

Stenfax bent his head. "Damn it, Gray."

Of course he should have known better than to believe Gray wouldn't tell Felicity about Elise at some point. Oh, he'd protect her from the salacious details, of course, but the siblings didn't keep secrets.

Sometimes they didn't speak of things. But they didn't keep secrets.

"Don't you dare blame him," Felicity croaked out. "I harangued it out of him and then I basically declared him to be a liar when he admitted the truth. But now I see this horrible thing he said is accurate." Tears filled her eyes and her voice was choked as she said, "How can this be true?"

He flinched at the sight of her pain. At the reminder that it wasn't only he who had been damaged by Elise's actions three years before.

"Felicity," he whispered, moving toward her. "Please."

She shook her head, backing away from him. "She betrayed you." Her fists clenched in and out at her sides. "She was my best friend and she betrayed *me*. How could you consider letting her back into your life, *our* lives? How could you think of going back to her?"

Stenfax shifted. In his attempts to not be crude, Gray had obviously left a great deal to the imagination.

"It is...it's not a courtship, Felicity," he whispered.

His sister had been married. Quite unhappily, of course, but

Jess Michaels

she had experienced a great deal more than the typical virginal miss. It took her a moment to digest what he said, to parse out its meaning, but when she did, her face twisted in disgust.

"Oh, Lucien," she breathed as she shook her head.

"It's complicated," he said, a weak defense of an indefensible position.

"I know complicated," she sobbed, tears flowing down her cheeks. "You don't even know how well acquainted I am with *complicated*, Lucien. But *this*?" She shook her head as she backed away from him toward the door. Her hands were raised as if in surrender. She reached behind her and opened the door, but before she left, she said, "Not this."

"Felicity," he said, but she turned and left, slamming the door.

He let out a painful bark as he slapped a palm against the closest flat surface. He leaned there for a moment, trying to block out the intense pain his actions had caused his sister. Felicity was often cool, she was sophisticated. It was easy to forget what she had endured in her life. How she had suffered before her husband had conveniently died in a drunken hunting accident.

She buried all that so deeply, not allowing anyone to speak to her about it. Losing Elise had only multiplied her pain.

And now he was dragging Felicity back through it because he couldn't keep his hands off Elise. He had to talk to his sister. He had to try to make her understand, to comfort her.

He spun around and stalked out the parlor door. He moved down the hall to the foyer swiftly and saw his sister getting into her carriage in the distance. She was gone before he could even call out to her and he let out a groan of disappointment.

But perhaps it was best to let her go for now. She would calm down and he would find a way to explain the unexplainable to her.

He moved to return to the ballroom, but before he could round the corner to the doors, there was a loud announcement from the entryway.

"The Duke of Kirkford and the Duchess of Kirkford."

Stenfax slowly turned the corner and watched as the new Duke of Kirkford enter the ballroom. And on his arm, dressed in a pink gown, was Elise.

CHAPTER SEVEN

Elise understood the concept of humiliation. In the past three years she had endured much of it. Her husband had been a happy extender of the feeling, reveling in her shame when he could create it.

Others had made her feel the sting as well. When she first entered Society as Duchess of Kirkford, there had been plenty of people who had cut her off for the scandalous breaking of her engagement to Stenfax. She had deserved that, she knew, and had taken it with her chin lifted as high as she could manage, even if she'd wept into her pillow at night at the shame.

But tonight, on display in a shocking gown, at a ball where she never should have been, out in company when the world thought she should be closeted in mourning, she had never experienced humiliation so completely.

The music no longer played in the room, everyone had turned toward her and they were whispering, their fans moving like butterfly wings as her name echoed on the air around her. Ambrose seemed immune to it all. In fact, he even seemed to enjoy it as he dragged her into the room.

She let her gaze move around those in attendance, hoping to find a friendly face. Instead, she found Grayson Danford, Stenfax's younger brother. His hard face was like steel as he glowered at her from his place with his new wife. Their mother was also in attendance, and even the flighty Lady Stenfax looked stunned to see her there.

None of the rest in the room gave her a smile or an

acknowledging wave and her heart sank. She was well and truly ruined at last. After years of spiraling toward that end, it was here.

But as the stunned silence hung on, the Marchioness of Swinton rushed forward, dragging a very bored Marquess with her. She made a huge show out of greeting Elise and Ambrose, though Elise couldn't have understood what she was saying if the lady had tattooed it across Elise's arm.

Because when she turned to greet the couple, she saw that Stenfax was now standing in the ballroom door behind her. Staring at her. His face filled with shock and horror. The crowd seemed to notice it, too, for they began to look back and forth between them. Waiting for...well, a showdown, Elise was certain. A scene.

In truth, she wasn't sure there wasn't about to *be* a scene. But then Stenfax sniffed and entered the room, passing her by like she wasn't even there as he moved over to where his family was standing.

That seemed to settle the room, for the music started again and the silence gave way to murmurs, though the stares went on. Lady Swinton sighed in relief as her party returned to something close to normal.

"Enjoy yourselves," she said, giving Elise a look that told her the marchioness wasn't an ally for her, either. Then she slipped back into the crowd with her husband, leaving Ambrose and Elise by the side of the dancefloor.

"I have some business to conduct," he said, releasing her arm at last. It felt like being released from a prison. "But you'll save a waltz for me later."

Elise pinched her lips together. "I shall not dance, Your Grace. It wouldn't be right. *None* of this is proper."

He leaned in. "Perhaps not. But I'd best not find you dancing with someone else, then. Or else you'll be walking home. In that dress, you won't make it."

He turned on his heel and left her standing there, well and truly caught by her circumstances. God, but she hated Ambrose.

She had hated Toby, as well. The cousins were two of a kind, raised entitled and cruel.

She knew very well just how cruel.

"Your Grace?"

Elise turned to find a gentleman approaching her. He was handsome in his own way, though he had an almost baby face. Probably because he had to be at least five years younger than her own six and twenty. His face also seemed familiar and she froze as she realized he was someone she'd seen circulating at Vivien's home.

"G-good evening," she stammered, praying this man wasn't about to out her. What a spectacle that would create. She'd never be able to leave her house again and what few acquaintances she might have left after this night would never speak to her after that.

He edged closer. "Forgive me for the forwardness, Your Grace. We have not been introduced."

She drew a few calming breaths. "But you know who I am."

"I do. You're the Duchess of Kirkford. And I am Theodore Winstead."

"The Viscount Winstead's youngest?" she asked, finding the information about his identity in the long list of names her mind somehow found space for.

He smiled. "That is me."

"A pleasure to make your acquaintance, Mr. Winstead," she said.

"The pleasure is all mine, I assure you, Your Grace." He shifted as if uncomfortable, and she saw how his gaze flitted to her cleavage, so heavily on display. She blushed even though this gown was meant exactly for that purpose.

Just not for here.

"Would you like to dance?" he asked.

She stiffened. To dance with him would only cause more consternation and possibly a great deal of trouble with Ambrose. So she shook her head. "I may not look it, but I'm still considered in mourning," she said, ducking her head in embarrassment. "It wouldn't be right."

He nodded slowly. "Then what about a turn around the terrace?"

She lifted her gaze to him. He did look very interested and there was nothing unkind about his face or his eyes. "Very well. It might be nice to escape the stifling warmth of this room."

He extended an arm and she took it, letting him lead her from the room. Outside a few couples and groups were gathered and most of them turned as the pair exited. Elise stiffened as the whispers from inside extended to the terrace.

A few shot her glares, then returned to the ballroom like she had a disease they might all catch. She released Mr. Winstead's arm and walked to the edge of the stone terrace.

"I have seen you before," Winstead said, coming up to lean against the terrace beside her. "I think you know where."

She refused to look at him as she gripped her fist against the scratchy stone. "I do. I've seen you there, as well. But you've never approached me. Why do it tonight when I'm a pariah?"

"You're popular at Vivien's," he explained. "And..."

He trailed off, and now she did turn toward him. "And?"

"And Lord Stenfax has seemed protective and interested. He isn't the kind of man one thwarts easily."

"You have no idea," Elise murmured as she looked once again at the dark garden below. "But you have the wrong notion. He is not interested. You saw him stalk past me without even a look tonight."

The young man nodded. "Yes, that action gave me the bravery to approach you at last."

Elise looked at him again. She felt nothing when she did so, not even a flutter of desire or interest. Yet she knew the Winstead family had money. This young man likely had means to keep a mistress if he wanted her. And there wasn't anything *unattractive* about him, exactly. He just wasn't...

Stenfax.

She frowned and drew a few long breaths, wishing she could press those thoughts of Lucien from her mind forever.

Wishing she could make all her memories go away and start fresh.

But she couldn't.

"If I approached you at Vivien's," Winstead continued. "Would you welcome that?"

She swallowed hard. "I would," she said, though the sound of the words was hollow. "I hope you will and we can get to know each other better there."

He smiled and looked even younger. Lord, she would rob a cradle before this was finished. What a ridiculous notion that was.

He took her hand and lifted it to his lips, pressing a brief kiss to her glove before he said, "I ought to go in. But I hope to see you again soon, Your Grace."

"Good night, Mr. Winstead," she said. "I'll stay here for a while."

He nodded and left her on the terrace. She looked around after he was gone. It seemed her unwanted presence had inspired all the others to leave, as well. It was just as well. She didn't think she could take more pointed stares and whispered insults tonight. If she could hide outside for a long enough time, perhaps she could find some way to convince Ambrose to allow her to go home.

She stared up at the sky with a sigh and a prayer for just that. The moon was just a sliver tonight and she looked up at that hint of beauty, focusing on it rather than her own awful circumstances.

"Elise."

At the sound of her name, she gripped her fist tighter on the stone. She didn't have to turn to know who had said it. But she did and caught her breath.

She'd seen Stenfax once tonight, but it didn't matter. Every time she looked at him, he took her breath away. He was as beautiful dressed formally as he was naked while he took her.

Well, *almost* as beautiful.

"You shouldn't be out here with me," she said, forcing

herself to look away. "I'm sure *they* are watching you."

He ignored the comment and took a long step toward her. "It doesn't matter. Elise, we need to talk."

Elise didn't respond to him immediately, and for that Stenfax was glad. It allowed him an extra moment to look at her, a tiny sparkle of moonlight bouncing off her luminous skin. Her dress was shocking, but it was beautiful. All that perfect flesh, teasing at more but not revealing it. It made a man want to glide his hands inside the folds of fabric and touch her until she shattered.

She licked her lips and he fought hard against the urge to do just that to her and more.

"Did you come out here to tell me that Mr. Winstead is evil?" she asked.

He frowned. Oh yes, he'd marked young Winstead's interest in Elise. Watching her walk outside with the man was one of the most difficult things he'd ever done. Harder still was not bursting out behind them and tossing the man into the bushes below.

"I have nothing negative to say about Winstead except that he's a pup," he said through clenched teeth.

She looked at him evenly, one fine eyebrow arching. "Well, he won't be forever, I suppose."

He shook his head. "No. I suppose not. Truly, I have never heard anything untoward about him."

She folded her arms. "Are you encouraging me to choose him as my protector then?"

"No," he whispered, trying to ignore the intense pain that ricocheted through him at that thought. The thought of someone like Winstead touching her. Giving her pleasure and having her return it. They were painful, erotic images that flooded his mind. "I could never do that."

"Why?" She turned away as she asked the question, but her pain was clear whether she faced him or not. It dripped from her voice, it sat on her rolled shoulders. "You don't want me. In fact, all this must thrill you."

"All this?" he repeated, uncertain what she meant.

Her shoulders bent further. "This idea that I am here in the height of humiliation. Being rejected by people I once called friend. Being forced to fuck for my freedom, my life."

He heard the wavering tears in her voice, even though she hadn't yet begun to weep outright. Suddenly he had a wild urge to take her in his arms, to take her away from this night and this life. To save her. To keep her.

But he couldn't do that. There was too much history between them. Still, he found himself moving toward her.

"None of those things give me any pleasure," he said as he reached out and placed a hand on her bare arm. She looked at it sitting there, her entire body shaking. "Once I wanted to hurt you. I wanted to make you feel the same brokenness I did when you left."

She lifted her gaze and a single tear escaped her eye, trailing down her cheek. She didn't move to wipe it away, but let it drag down to her chin.

"Oh, Lucien," she whispered. "I did. I assure you, I did."

He caught his breath. There was something so real in what she said. Like she had truly suffered for her choices, the same way he had suffered for them.

"Elise," he whispered.

But she looked past him rather than letting him in. She looked toward the house, and he saw her face crumple even further. "I see that Kirkford is looking for me," she said. "Goodnight, Lucien."

She pulled from his touch and walked away without a backward glance. He watched her go, incapable of following, incapable of stopping her.

But when she was gone, he at last caught his breath. There was something more going on here. Something more than he had ever understood before. And now he wanted to know what that was. He wanted the answers he'd never dared seek before, ones he thought he'd known all these years.

But he had no idea if that search would send him spiraling out of control...or send him home to the only woman who had ever held his heart.

Elise sat stiffly in Ambrose's carriage as they made their way home. She had been lucky the new duke had suffered a headache that had forced them from the ball early.

Still, she couldn't stop thinking of Stenfax on the terrace. He had reached out to her and she had said too much, she had tried to make some kind of excuse for herself. She had told him of her suffering. As if that mattered. She had done what she'd done. The why of it wouldn't help anyone.

"Well, Elise," Ambrose said, drawing her attention to him, away from the troubling thoughts of her encounter with Stenfax. "I hope tonight has helped you understand how very alone you are now."

She pinched her lips and fought the urge to bark out a humorless laugh. Somehow she didn't think this feckless buffoon would appreciate that. "I already knew that, Ambrose, I assure you."

He leaned closer, and he was all but looking down her dress as he did so. "You don't have to be in a precarious position, Elise. You could stay right in your home, you could even find yourself with a bit of pin money again. You just have to give *me* something in return."

Elise's stomach turned. And there it was, spoken out loud at last. Ambrose wanted her to be his mistress. And wasn't that what she was looking for herself, a powerful protector? Except the very idea of bedding her hated husband's equally hated cousin was disgusting beyond measure. The street itself was more appealing.

The carriage pulled into her drive and Elise edged toward the door. "Let me make this clear to you, Ambrose. No. Never. I would *never* trade myself for your house and your protection. Good night."

She fled the carriage before he could react, but she heard his salty curse, hurtled at her as the carriage pulled away into the darkness.

For a moment, she stood in her drive, trying to calm herself, trying to catch her breath. But it was impossible. Ambrose was right that tonight had proven just how alone she was in the world.

And it had also shown her that being alone was more dangerous now than ever. She had to move forward with her plan to escape this man, this house, and to escape the tangled feelings that Stenfax inspired in her.

Ones that would lead to nothing but more pain and more ruin for them both.

CHAPTER EIGHT

Stenfax swung off his horse and looked up at his mother's London home as a groom came rushing down to take his mount. He let out a long sigh. He wasn't looking forward to this. But it had to be done.

Her butler opened the door as Lucien came up the steps two by two. "Good afternoon, my lord," he said, taking Stenfax's hat and gloves.

"Hello Riley," he said. "Are my mother and sister in residence?"

"They're taking tea in the west parlor, my lord. Shall I announce you?"

"No need," Stenfax said, smiling at the man before he moved down the hall.

He heard their voices as he approached. Their mother, soft and slightly silly, Felicity's voice bright and intelligent. As he entered the chamber, both of them turned, and there were two reactions. His mother's face lit up with pleasure, Felicity's tightened with pain and caution.

"Good afternoon," Stenfax said as his mother hurried over. He pressed a kiss to her cheek. "Oh, it looks like I've come just at the end of tea."

Lady Stenfax shook her head. "I'll call for more. We'd love to have you, wouldn't we Felicity?"

Felicity got to her feet and faced Stenfax fully, her hands folded in front of her. "If that is what the earl desires. It seems he does whatever he'd like anyway."

Their mother jerked her face toward Felicity. "What are you talking about?"

Stenfax glared at Felicity and then patted his mother's arm reassuringly. "We had a little disagreement last night, Mama, nothing more. I came to talk to Felicity, actually. Perhaps we could go to the music room and chat?"

Felicity shrugged. "As you like."

"Before you go, may I speak to you a moment, Lucien?" their mother asked.

Felicity exchanged a look with him, then said, "I'll meet you down the hall."

She left, and their mother turned into him, searching his face with worry. "Are you well, darling?"

He wrinkled his brow. He loved his mother dearly, but no one could say she was the most observant woman in the world. She had once been described as flighty, and that was certainly true.

"I'm fine, Mama. I assure you," he said. Lied, actually, for he didn't feel fine.

"I-I saw the Duchess of Kirkford at the ball last night," she continued. "I suppose *everyone* saw her."

Stenfax stiffened. "Yes, there was quite the stir regarding her."

She squeezed his arm. "I hope that doesn't pain you."

He considered the question. Pain him? To see Elise? Hell yes, it pained him. But surprisingly it wasn't because of the betrayal or the lies or the abandonment.

It hurt to see her because he couldn't touch her freely. He couldn't stop her from talking to men like Winstead and planning a future that would include him no more than her past had.

"No," he said softly. "Whatever was between us is in the past, isn't it? I can't *allow* it to hurt me."

His mother took his words at face value and nodded before she said, "Best go talk to Felicity, then. Good afternoon, Lucien."

He smiled at her before he left the room. It was easy to get her to believe him. Felicity would be harder. No one would dare call *her* flighty.

He walked down the hall and into the music room. Felicity stood at the window, overlooking the garden behind the house. When he entered the room and closed the door, she turned on him, her face taut with the same powerful emotions she had displayed the night before.

"I couldn't leave things as they were," he said. "I wanted to discuss what happened last night."

She shrugged, and he could tell this would not be easy. "I'm not sure there's anything to discuss. After all, you seem to have made up your mind, despite the past. Despite what that past nearly drove you to do."

He flinched. She was referencing that night on the terrace. That night he'd nearly taken his own life. Of course she knew about that night—Gray had told her. Stenfax had always known that.

"Please," he said softly, moving toward her. "Let's not discuss that."

She threw up her hands in exasperation. "Of course. We never discuss *that*. Even though it's the most horrible thing that nearly happened to us. Even though it changed Gray forever, changed you forever, and changed *me* forever."

"You weren't there, Felicity," he said, trying to be calm when this topic made him anything but.

"I think that made it worse," Felicity said, stepping toward him. "I think it was worse to know you nearly killed yourself and that I wasn't there to try to stop you. Do you know how many times I went over the last thing I'd said to you before that night? Do you know what my last words to you would have been had you succeeded in ending yourself?"

"What were they?" Stenfax asked.

She blinked at tears. He was shocked to see them a second time, for Felicity had hardly ever cried after her husband's death. She'd become stronger than iron after that night.

"I said, 'will you hand me the salt'."

He wrinkled his brow. "What?"

"The last time I saw you before you climbed a terrace wall was at supper the night before. I asked you to pass me the salt but we didn't talk again. I had a headache and I snuck out. So the last thing I would have said to my eldest brother, who I adore beyond measure, was something about *salt*."

He swallowed hard. "I'm sorry, Felicity. Just as I'm sorry that this thing with Elise stirs such painful memories for you."

"It does," she admitted. "And *regrets*. I have also often thought of what I would have said to you had I faced you in your grief on the terrace that night. Would you like to know what I decided those words would have been?"

He slowly nodded, though this entire conversation was an exercise in intense pain.

She reached out and caught his hands with hers. "I would have told you that there were some nights during my marriage when jumping from a terrace to end the pain also appealed to me. That I understood the impulse because I'd felt it too."

He drew back. He'd known how terrible Felicity's marriage had been. Both he and Gray had tried to extract her from Viscount Barbridge's clutches, but she was legally bound to him. They had seen her bruises, seen her brokenness, and been helpless to save her.

But to know she had considered the same bitter end he had was heart-wrenching.

"But you didn't," he said. "And I'm glad neither of us took that path."

"As am I," she whispered. "But now I'm terrified for you. I know you loved Elise. Truly loved her with all your heart. I know that losing her once was nearly unbearable. If you entangle yourself with her again, you *know* it won't work out."

He shut his eyes. Yes, that was true. There was no happy end here. That was *his* choice now. Even if Elise drew him in like a moth to a dancing, beautiful flame.

"I know it won't," he admitted.

"And the closer you get, the more painful that end will be. I don't want to see her tear you apart again. I don't want to see her hurt you. To see you hurt yourself. So if I am harsh with you, that's why. It's out of fear. Fear for your safety and for your very life."

"Felicity, I love you with all my heart for your concern," he said, drawing her in to kiss her forehead and feeling her shudder at this massive display of emotion that she normally kept tucked tightly inside.

"Then tell me how to stop fearing what will happen to you," she whispered.

He moved her to the settee and they sat together. He smiled at her even though it hurt. Everything hurt. She was making him face a truth, and a consequence, of these actions.

He sighed. "You must understand that things are different now. Part of why I was so devastated three years ago was that I believed *Elise* to be someone different. I know what she's capable of now."

He said those words, but the moment he did, he realized how little they rang true. He'd believed her to be no better than a demon for so long, but in the past few weeks since they'd been thrown into each other's path again, he had seen no evidence of that. She hadn't made any attempt to excuse what she'd done.

She'd just been…herself.

He shook his head and forced himself to continue, "I suppose I mean that I don't have any expectations that we could be together, or that anything she says can be trusted. I won't allow myself to be hurt. Not again."

Felicity lifted her gaze to his. "You say that, Lucien, but the past has come back. You think you can control everything that comes along with it, but…"

"But?"

"You may not be able to." She turned away. "I know if someone I loved and had lost suddenly resurfaced in my life, I would have a difficult time facing it."

Lucien pinched his lips. Felicity hadn't had any long-lost

loves that he knew of, despite how her voice was filled with regret. But she made a good point. Emotions had been stirred now. He couldn't pretend that there weren't potential dangers to the line he had been walking.

"I'll be careful," he vowed. "I won't let anything happen that I'll lament later."

"I hope that's true, Lucien. I've lost too much in my life to fathom losing you."

He squeezed her hand gently. "You won't. I promise." He pushed to his feet and drew her up with him. "Now, why don't we go see if Mama wants to take a walk in the garden before I go? I know how she loves to show me her roses."

Felicity nodded, but Stenfax still saw the hesitation in her gaze. The uncertainty and fear about his future and his choices. As he led her out of the room, he couldn't blame her.

In truth, he was beginning to feel the same way about what he was doing with Elise. And he wondered if he would survive unscathed and unchanged when he finally found the strength to walk away.

CHAPTER NINE

Elise sat at a table in the far corner of Vivien's club, staring at the room around her. The scene was still shocking, but the more times she returned to this place, the less shocked she found herself feeling. Watching the others engage in their erotic games was sometimes embarrassing, but sometimes titillating. And sometimes she didn't even notice them at all.

She supposed it was good she was becoming accustomed to such things. There was no use in being naïve anymore. She had to commit fully to this endeavor at last. Ambrose's scene after the ball just two nights ago had proven that to be true.

She cast her gaze around the room one more time, but this time she wasn't looking at naked flesh and grinding motions. No, this time she looked at faces, especially the faces of the women in the crowd. Many looked happy, aroused, totally engaged in whatever they were doing and whoever they were with.

Others, though, had a hollow look to them. An emptiness.

Elise frowned. She would be one of the empty ones. That much was becoming very clear.

"May I join you?"

Elise glanced up to find Vivien Manning standing beside her. She was wearing a shocking gown with a gauzy top that left very little to the imagination. Yet she somehow she still managed a cool sophistication that Elise envied.

"Certainly," Elise said, motioning the chair beside her. "I would appreciate the company."

Vivien settled into the chair and looked around her with a sigh. "We are a busy group tonight."

"You always seem to be. That must give you pleasure."

"It gives me money," Vivien said with a small, rather sad smile. "Though I do enjoy many of the games played here."

"Did you always?"

Vivien shot her a side glance. "No," she admitted. "When I first became a mistress, it wasn't easy. It got better as time went on and I found protectors who were kind and patient."

Elise nodded slowly. "I sincerely hope for the same. It would make this easier."

"Still, it helps to know what you want," Vivien said, leaning in.

A vision of Lucien rose up in Elise's mind. Not just Lucien as she'd had him lately, angry and passionate, but the person she'd known as a girl. The one she'd loved for so long she could hardly recall a time when she hadn't. The Lucien who had once whispered how deeply he loved her and wanted her in his life for the rest of his days.

She caught her breath. "I want independence and protection and—"

"You want him," Vivien interrupted.

Elise stopped talking and tried not to look at the courtesan directly. "I don't know what you're talking about. There are many *hims* at present."

"Then I shall be more specific. You want Stenfax," Vivien said softly.

Elise bent her head. She had been fighting to be strong for so long. Fighting to deny what she felt in her heart so that it didn't overwhelm her and send her into a dark place where she feared she'd never escape. She had been trying not to slip into despair as she considered a future she'd never have.

"He doesn't want me," she murmured.

Vivien let out a soft chuckle. "My billiard table would beg to differ."

Heat filled Elise's cheeks as she pictured that intense night with Lucien not so very long ago. She had no idea their joining had been so closely marked.

"I'm sorry," she said.

Vivien covered her arm gently. "My dear, I was not seeking an apology. This place is meant for pleasure. Anyway and anywhere you can find it."

Elise allowed herself to look at Vivien fully. "You have been doing this a long time now."

Vivien nodded. "I have."

"How do you keep from involving your emotions?"

Vivien's expression suddenly darkened and her eyes grew sad for a brief moment. "Sometimes you don't," she whispered.

Elise stared at her, sensing there was a great deal more to this woman than perhaps she'd guessed. She shook her head. "But *I* must," she continued, leaving Vivien to her private emotions since she assumed the other woman would never share them. "With Stenfax especially because he can't overlook his rage over what I did to him."

"Have you ever told him why?" Vivien asked, her tone low and surprisingly gentle.

Elise shook her head. "I've thought of doing so a dozen times, but it feels cheap to do it now. It doesn't change what I did. It would only bring him so much more pain. It would bring everyone much more pain."

Vivien tilted her head. "You're punishing yourself."

Elise caught her breath. She'd never thought of it in those terms before, but now she recognized them as the absolute truth. "Perhaps," she admitted. "Perhaps I deserve to suffer as I made him suffer."

"I would wager you've been punished enough," Vivien said.

Tears swelled in Elise's eyes and she blinked to keep them from falling. "Ask Lucien if that's true. I'm certain he will tell you I haven't paid half my penance yet."

Vivien's gaze slid away from her face to a point behind her and she smiled softly. "It seems you could ask him yourself. He just came in and he's obviously looking for you."

Elise spun in her chair to look at the door behind her. Indeed, Lucien was there, beautiful as always, scanning the room. When his eyes found her, there was a moment when pleasure crossed his face and he looked just as he had when he still loved her. The tears she'd forced not to fall returned and one trailed its way down her cheek before she wiped it away.

"Don't throw away hope, Your Grace," Vivien said as she pushed to her feet. "Good luck."

Stenfax let his gaze move over the room in Vivien's club, ignoring the writhing bodies and moaning couples, and instantly found Elise. She was sitting at a table with Vivien and he couldn't help but smile. She wasn't with some gentleman. She wasn't offering herself to a protector.

In that moment, he thought of Felicity and his smile fell. His feelings were exactly what she feared. That he was giving himself over to emotions that would only damage him and the people he loved.

In that same moment, he knew he had to end what he had foolishly started with Elise. Before he loved her again. Before he lost her again. Before he tore his own heart out and damaged it beyond repair.

He felt sick as he moved toward her. He watched as Vivien got up from her place and turned toward him. Her little smile as she passed him made him realize she and Elise were likely discussing him, and that made it all the worse somehow.

Elise stood as he reached her table, her face a combination of welcome and wariness. "Good evening, my lord," she said, her voice catching a fraction.

He fought the urge to reach for her and nodded. "Elise, I—" he began, and couldn't find the words. He wasn't going to do this out here. It wasn't right. "Would you come with me?"

There was a moment when all her pain, all her fear, all her hesitation flowed over her face like a waterfall. But she reined it in, of course she did, and nodded. "If you'd like," she whispered.

He didn't touch her, mostly because he feared what would happen if he did. He merely turned and started off across the room with her walking behind him. At the hallway, he murmured what he wanted to one of the men who worked for Vivien and he gave Stenfax a key to a room.

He moved down the hall, ignoring the sounds of pleasure that pierced into the narrow space, taunting him, arousing him. He stopped at a chamber and unlocked it, letting her in past him, her sweet scent swirling up around him as she did.

He locked the door behind himself to give them privacy and turned to face her. She stood in the middle of the room, just in front of the bed, her hands clenched in front of her. She looked like she was being taken to the gallows and he briefly wondered if she could read his mind...if she knew his thoughts thanks to his face or his posture.

Once upon a time she'd been able to do that, or so it seemed. But that was a lifetime ago.

"Elise, I need to talk to you," he began.

She swallowed hard, and for the first time he saw how tired she looked. How wrung dry by everything she was doing. It swept away his intentions and he moved toward her a step even though he knew there was no prudence in the action.

"Why are you doing this?"

Her face crumpled when he said it, and she caught her breath on a wavering sob. "You keep asking me that. Over and over, no matter how many times I give you the answer. I know you have every reason to doubt me, but am I so evil that you think everything is a lie? Even my deepest and darkest pain?"

He drew back at the emotional display. Elise had kept her feelings so close in, never revealing much beyond her pleasure since the moment he'd first seen her again. To see anger, pain, desperation now...it was like he'd opened a book and found the girl he once knew all those years ago.

It was like he saw the real her.

"Elise—"

"No!" She held up a shaking hand. "I understand you have every right to despise me. To punish me. To want to see me suffer. But I do, Lucien. I do suffer. And I'm doing the best I can in a situation that is so terrifying I can hardly express it to you. So if you came to batter me about my motives for seeking a protector, then I..." She caught her breath and spun away. "*I can't.*"

He moved to her even though he shouldn't. He just couldn't stop himself. He slipped behind her, wrapping his arms around her, feeling her tremble as he pulled her against him. She didn't fight him. In fact, she went almost limp, like she needed him to prop her up as she drew in harsh breath after harsh breath.

He turned her gently, folding her into his arms as she clenched a fist against his chest, her cheek coming to rest there. For what seemed like forever, they stood like that. He smoothed her hair gently as she clung to him.

And it was like no time had passed. She lifted her face and he stared into it, seeing the future they once would have had. The future snatched away by her decisions. But for the first time, he didn't blame her for that.

He just mourned what they had both lost.

He slid a hand into hair, tilting her face even more. Then he lowered his mouth to hers and gently kissed her. She made a soft sound in her throat, something on the brink between pleasure and pain. Something that spoke volumes in the language of their relationship.

He pressed his tongue to her lips and she opened for him easily, taking him in, welcoming him. There was no desperation, just a gentle caress. And in that moment he wanted to make love to her.

Not claim her. Not fuck her. Not punish her with pleasure.

He wanted to make love to her.

Wordlessly, he let his fingers splay against her back, finding the buttons along her spine. She deepened the kiss as he

83

loosened her gown, spread the fabric open and finally stepped away from her to silently draw the bodice away from her body. She, too, was silent as she stared into his eyes. It was as if they both feared that words would shatter this spell between them. Break this bubble where no damage had ever torn them apart.

He lowered the dress around her hips and she shimmied, shuffling it past the gentle swell until it fell in a circle around her feet. Of course she wore nothing beneath. Just as she'd worn nothing beneath every single time he'd come to her here.

He was glad of it. That meant there was more time to look at her in all her beauty. To worship rather than unwrap the gift that was her touch and her taste and her feel.

He pressed his fingers into her hair, combing away the pins that held it in place, letting long, thick locks of reddish gold fall all around them like a curtain. Her hair smelled like lemons and jasmine and he sucked in that scent to hold it inside of him.

He guided her backward until her thighs hit the high bed. He lifted her onto the edge and they were face to face again. He cupped her cheeks, smoothing his thumbs along the contours, and kissed her once more. She tasted like sweet honey and sharp liquor, she tasted like the thing he craved most.

And he wanted to taste her everywhere tonight.

He drew away from her mouth and gently placed his hands on her shoulders to push her onto her back. She went without argument, resting back on the bed with a sigh like she hadn't been able to find peace like this for a long time.

Neither had he. He climbed up beside her, turning her until her head rested on the pillows. She stared up at him, waiting, silent, surrendering.

He pressed a kiss to her lips and she lifted her hands to his hair, sliding the edges of her fingernails against his scalp, angling his head for a deeper kiss that seemed to go on forever.

He finally managed to slide away, dragging his mouth along her chin, her throat, her shoulder. She shivered in response, whispering out an incoherent sound of pleasure. That little sound rocked through him, setting him on fire as much as her touch or her taste did. It awoke something in him he hadn't allowed to live for a long time.

The desire to give to her, entirely and completely. And though he knew he was a fool, though he knew nothing could change in the long term due to their history, tonight he would surrender to that desire.

Surrender to her.

He moved his lips over the swell of her breast and she gasped as he stroked his tongue over one nipple. It hardened beneath the touch, rising to meet him like she would when he entered her body. He sucked there, feeling her shift beneath him, reaching for and trying to escape intense pleasure as she tugged at his hair with ragged, helpless cries.

He smiled against her skin and moved his attention to the other nipple, repeating the pull and tug, the slide of wet against hard until she was gasping for breath.

He moved lower then, rubbing his cheek against her smooth, flat stomach, holding her hips steady while he sucked a path lower and lower. She lifted toward him, offering herself out of instinct, but he ignored the ultimate goal of her slick sex and instead glided lower, pulling at her stocking with his teeth, rolling it away with his hands.

He repeated the action on the other leg and now she was truly naked, truly his. She sat up on her elbows to watch him, her gaze fully focused and fully aware of the power of this moment, just as he was.

He never looked away as he slid his hands back up her legs. He never looked away as he pressed against her thighs and she opened to him with a shudder. He never looked away even as he slid his fingers up the inside of her leg and finally touched the sweet hidden jewel of her pussy.

Only when he felt the slick wetness there did he allow himself to look down at the apex of her legs. She opened them a little wider, unashamed of his attention, welcoming it as she would welcome him.

And he was ready to take her. Eager. Only not yet. First, he wanted something else. He leaned down, settling between her legs, spreading her open with both hands. She shivered, whispering his name, her hands gripping the coverlet near her hips.

He ignored her begging. He ignored everything except for the sweet treat before him. Finally, he leaned in and darted his tongue out to taste her, and she let out a cry that certainly echoed in the room, likely echoed in the hall. A cry that made his cock jolt beneath his trousers.

A cry that signaled it was only the beginning of this night. And he couldn't wait to do more to make that sound escape her lips again.

CHAPTER TEN

Elise gasped, searching for air and finding none as Lucien settled his hot mouth against her trembling sex. She couldn't believe he was doing this, touching her like this, loving her like this. No one had ever done it before.

And yet now it felt like this was what she'd been waiting for her entire life. This feeling of sharp pleasure, this intense sensation of being loved rather than being merely claimed.

It was amazing, and she cried out helplessly as he stroked his rough tongue along the entire length of her weeping slit. The sensation was incredible, focused and powerful, sharp and so pleasurable that she began to tremble almost immediately.

He took his time, holding her open with one hand while he licked and licked, leaving no part of her safe from his attentions. She found her hips moving to greet him, grinding against him to strengthen the already intensely powerful pleasure building in her.

He smiled against her skin, looking up at her as he claimed her and the power of their gazes meeting made the experience even more intense.

He began to focus his wicked tongue more and more on her clitoris. His licks there becoming harder, his attentions lasting longer, and finally he began to suck her gently, then harder. As he did so, he slid one finger into her sheath, curling it slowly.

Concentrated sensation rushed through her veins, her bones, her every fiber, and she twisted her head against the pillows, lost to the throbbing need that coursed through her trembling body. And then, with an expert combination of mouth and fingers, he thrust her over the edge.

She had never experienced pleasure like this. The waves were deep and never ending, jolts that kept coming and coming so long as he suckled at her twitching body. And it went on and on, until she felt lost, until she felt found all over again.

Finally, he stroked his tongue over her one last time and withdrew his finger gently. She found her breath at last just as he pushed from the bed. She watched him, dazed, as he stripped out of his clothing in front of the firelight. He was smiling at her as he did it, clearly enjoying the results of his earlier handiwork.

She reached for him and he let her catch his hand. He moved forward, taking his place back on the bed. Only this time he covered her with his body, settling between her legs, his arms braced on the coverlet as he looked down at her.

He said nothing, but nothing needed to be said. She saw everything in his eyes. Everything she had loved about him, everything she had lost. She saw the future she'd once planned with him, the one that had been shattered all those years ago by impossible circumstances out of her control.

She reached for him, touching his cheek, his shoulders, smoothing her hands along his warm flesh as if to prove this all wasn't some dream. If it was, she wanted to stay in it forever.

Even if she knew that wasn't possible.

His expression shifted, as if he read some version of her thoughts. His lips drew down into a frown and he leaned in to kiss her. She wrapped her arms around his neck, clinging to him, and gasped as he slid his cock deep inside her in one long thrust.

He held still for a moment, just kissing her, like he wanted to really feel her body, feel this moment. She did the same, flexing around his hardness, curling her fingers against the planes of muscle on his back. This moment, if nothing else, was hers.

She would remember it for the rest of her days.

He began to move then, slow thrusts that began to rebuild the fire he had created with his mouth earlier. He drew back from her as he did so, watching her as he took her.

She lifted to meet him, grinding against his pelvis, taking all the pleasure she could from him. He shuddered, making a low sound in his throat that was better than any pretty words he might have concocted.

He also shifted, rolling onto his back so that she was on top of him. She sat up, adjusting herself onto her knees. Now she had the power and it was amazing to feel that way. Especially considering how much taking Stenfax had done since their reunion. Oh, she'd loved it, but now this was her pleasure, *her* taking.

She wasn't going to waste it. She reached down and grabbed his hands, pressing them back against the pillows, tangling her fingers in hers. She rolled her hips over his, watching how his face twitched with pleasure. The same pleasure echoed in her body.

She wanted to make this last all night. Something screamed at her to draw it out, but it was difficult when her body reached for pleasure and found it in spades. Her thrusts grew faster as she neared release a second time and then she was falling over the edge again. She worked her spasming body over his, hard and fast, crying out with release and relief that she couldn't control.

His neck strained as she did so, and once again he flipped her over onto her back. He moved against her with hard, heavy thrusts that only served to draw out her own pleasure even more. Finally, his face twisted, his breath grew harsh and he cried out her name and pulled away from her. The proof of his release splashed across the sheets and her stomach as he came.

As his breathing slowed, he looked down at he and she saw the moment his feelings changed. There was a slow tension that entered his face as he looked at her. A wall that came down between them.

And it tore into her. Earlier in the night, she had confessed her pain and he'd comforted her. More than that, he'd made love to her, *really* made love to her. She'd had a tiny hope that maybe that meant something.

But she could see now that it didn't.

"Let me get you a handkerchief," he said, speaking to her like she was nothing but an acquaintance who had sneezed.

She sat up as he got off the bed and swept up his trousers. He put them on before he caught his waistcoat and pulled a folded square from the pocket. He held it out and she stared at it.

"No," she said. "I don't want it."

He wrinkled his brow. "Don't you want to clean yourself up?"

She let out a broken laugh. "I'm not dirty, Lucien. I have no need for it. I'm a woman who just shared something wonderful with her lover. I feel no need to wipe away the evidence, nor to pretend this night away. Not like you."

He turned his face, breaking off their connection once more. "Elise."

She pursed her lips at the exasperation in his voice. There was no arguing with it. They were stuck in this loop, it seemed. He despised her but couldn't resist her. He would take her and yet never allow these moments to soften his heart.

Meanwhile, every single moment they shared tattooed his name on her very soul.

She gathered the coverlet and flopped it over herself for some kind of protection. "You got what you came for, Stenfax," she said softly. "Of course you'll go. The easier to forget you've sunk so low."

He let out a low, pained sound and she jerked her face toward him to find that he had dropped the waistcoat back at his feet and was just staring at her.

"Is that what you think?" he said. "That I come here, I fuck you and I go home without a thought for you?"

She shrugged. "It's hard to think that isn't true based on what I've experienced."

He moved toward her a long step, his hands shaking at his sides, his eyes flashing with emotion. "You know nothing, Elise.

Not a damn thing."

"Then explain it to me," she barked, sliding to the edge of the bed, the covers wrapped around her. "Explain it. God, just say *anything* that means something."

"I don't leave here and forget you," he growled. "I have tried so very hard to do just that over the years, but it never works. For three years, I have woken up with one thought in my head. Do you know what that thought is?"

She shook her head wordlessly, for she was honestly afraid to say anything for fear her voice would make him truncate his confession.

"Elise is gone," he said softly, almost tenderly. "I wake up every morning with that thought in my head. I go to bed each night with the same fucking thought echoing so loudly that it almost blocks out every other thing. I eat my breakfast, Elise is gone. I go to my club, Elise is gone. I try so bloody hard to move on, but *Elise is gone.*"

She sucked in a hard, harsh breath not just at his words, but at the crumpled pain on his face when he said them. "I'm sorry," she whispered.

"I've tried *everything* I could think of to dismiss you from my mind, Elise. I even tried to seek out a marriage."

She flinched. "Yes, I know."

God, how that had burned her to the ground when she heard Stenfax was engaged to be married again. She'd even gone so far as to find out where the lady in question—Celia Fitzgilbert—lived, just to see her. And she'd hated her, briefly, for being so pretty.

But then the engagement had ended, right around the time Elise's own husband had died and it was like all the lights in the world had been lit at once.

"Do you want to know why my engagement to Celia ended?" he asked.

"I-I heard it was because Gray fell in love with her sister. That you two stepped aside so that they could wed."

He sighed, a sound of pure exhaustion with it all. "Gray *did*

91

fall in love with Rosalinde. But that's not why. Celia and I ended our engagement because there was no feeling between us. She wasn't willing to sacrifice a future with love and I wasn't going to make her. She recently married someone she does love, so I am happy I let her go."

"And you?" she whispered.

He laughed, but it was empty. "Me? Well, I took a great deal of time to analyze that subject after the end of the engagement. And I've come to realize that there is no feeling left in me, Elise. You took it all when you left."

She pushed to her feet, now dragging just the sheet behind her. "No, you can't mean that."

He nodded. "But I do. I have *no* love left. I have no capacity for the kind that a wife desires and requires. I have nothing left because *Elise is gone.*"

A sound cracked through the air and she realized with a start that it was her own moan of anguish at his words. The depth of his pain was so deep and so dark, and she had caused it. She had ripped his heart out and hadn't even known she'd been carrying it with her all this time. How she hated herself for that.

But it also gave her a tiny sense of...hope. If Lucien had been so broken by her, did it mean she could repair him as well? Repair *them?* After all, he kept coming to her despite these hard and harsh feelings. He kept wanting her despite his better judgment.

Didn't that count for something?

She reached for him. He didn't back away as she gently placed a hand on his heart.

"Couldn't we..." She drew a long breath. It took so much to say this, to ask it. "Couldn't we start over?"

He went almost impossibly still for what felt like forever. He stared at her, his dark gaze filled with such heartbreak that it was physically painful. Then he reached up and took the hand that rested on his chest. He threaded his fingers through hers and held it, gently.

"Elise," he whispered. "You are temptation embodied and

not just because of what we share in bed. But I can't trust you. I don't know that I *ever* could again, no matter what you said or did to try to prove to me that I could."

She bit back a cry. There it was. The final nail in her hopes and in her heart. If this man didn't trust her, *couldn't* trust her, then none of the rest mattered.

And yes, she could explain herself. But what she had said to Vivien earlier in the night now felt truer than ever. Her words would be meaningless. She couldn't change what had happened, nor take away the pain this man had experienced in the interim because of her.

If she told him the truth, it would be as some kind of absolution for herself. It wouldn't make him trust her, it would only hurt him and others even more.

To confess would be a selfish act.

"I understand," she whispered when she could find her voice, find her words, find a way not to break down when she spoke.

He let go of her hand and instead reached out to cup her cheek. His fingers caressed her skin far more gently than she deserved considering what he'd just told her.

"We can't do this anymore, can we?" he asked.

She bit back a sob. "No. No, I think it hurts us both too much."

He leaned in, his mouth a breath from hers. "Then we must make tonight special. A better goodbye than our last one."

She squeezed her eyes shut, tears escaping no matter how she fought them. Then she opened them and looked at him. "Yes," she whispered, and cupped his face to draw him to her lips.

He kissed her, gently, sweetly, as he backed her toward the bed once more. And as they fell together, she pushed away all her pain, all her awareness that this night had now transformed into a goodbye. She would have plenty of time later to deal with that reality. For now she just wanted to have this last moment with him.

This last moment with the man she loved more than anything in this world.

CHAPTER ELEVEN

"The Marquess and Marchioness of Folworth to see you, my lord."

Stenfax lifted his head from the line of figures he had been staring at, unseeing, for several hours to find his butler Xavier at the door. He shook his head.

"Of course. Show them to the parlor."

The servant bowed and backed from the room, leaving Stenfax to collect himself. And collect himself he would have to do. It had been three days since he last saw Elise and he hadn't been sleeping, he'd hardly eaten.

How had he survived three years like this? He could hardly remember.

He kept wanting to go to Vivien's. To find Elise there and just have one more night. It took every fiber of his being not to do just that.

"It's over," he reminded himself before he got up and walked to the parlor where his friends awaited him.

He stepped inside and found Folly and Marina standing together at the fire. They turned in unison as he shut the door, and Folly tilted his head. "Christ, you look like hell."

Marina slapped his arm. "Folly!"

"It's true," Folly said with a shrug. "I imagine he knows it."

"But I always appreciate the reminder," Stenfax said in a dry tone as he motioned to the settee. "Would you like tea?"

They both shook their heads and everyone sat, Folly and Marina on the settee, Stenfax in a chair across from them. "It's nice to see you," he said. "Regardless of my appearance. I had actually forgotten we had planned this meeting today. My apologies."

Marina leaned forward. She was a beautiful woman, with sharp green eyes that flitted over his face and read him in an instant. "You wanted to know about the Duke of Kirkford. The *new* duke, I suppose."

"Yes," he said with a short nod. "I already know everything I ever wanted to know about the last one."

Both Folly and Marina frowned. Folly was the one who spoke. "I assume this means the rumors of your...*reconnecting* to Elise are true?"

Stenfax stiffened. Folly had been a friend for years, and he trusted Marina implicitly. But he couldn't spill everything in his heart to them any more than he was able to do so with Gray. All three of them were too involved. Too biased.

"It was nothing," he lied. "A brief dalliance with an old flame. It's...it's over now."

Marina pressed her lips together and it was clear she didn't fully believe him. "And yet you still wish to know about the new duke."

Stenfax shifted. He should probably say no. He should probably *mean* no. After all, if he and Elise were over, he had no cause to involve himself in her life. She intended to take a protector, after all, and it would be that man's position to defend her if she needed it.

And yet he didn't say no.

"I was merely curious about him," Stenfax said. "Especially after that scene when he dragged Elise to the ball despite her still being in mourning."

Marina flinched. "Ah yes. That was a dreadful night. The gossips are still chewing over that. They'll work the marrow from that bone for a long time to come."

Stenfax swallowed hard. Elise would likely not survive socially, it seemed. Once upon a time he would have been happy for that. Now he felt a strange urge to protect her from the consequences.

Not that he could.

"You know that Felicity had…troubles with her husband," Stenfax said softly. "A certain kind of trouble. I simply want to ensure the man isn't abusing Elise in any way. As I would if I suspected such a thing from *any* man in my acquaintance."

Folly cocked his head with an incredulous expression. "Certainly. It has *nothing* to do with your past engagement to the woman and your present…dalliance."

"Not present," Stenfax reminded him. Reminded himself.

Marina sighed. "If you are determined, then I can tell you little good about Ambrose. He and our other cousin Roger were born on the very same day, so when Toby died, the two of them went to absolute war over the title. Both of them are cruel bullies, just as the last duke was."

Stenfax nodded. As much as he'd tried to steer clear of information regarding the inheritance of the hated title of Duke of Kirkford earlier in the year, he did know all that.

"But do you think he would…harm Elise?" he pressed.

Marina exchanged a look with Folly. "All my cousins are cruel," she said softly. "And certainly capable of terrible things. I always suspected that Ambrose was jealous of Toby, of his marriage to Elise. And Toby flaunted it, flaunted *her* like a prize he'd won. I wouldn't doubt that Ambrose is pursuing some kind of vile interest in her now that she's a widow, but to physically harm her…I just don't know, Stenfax."

This was not comforting. He gripped the chair arms hard enough that he felt them creak beneath his fists.

When he was silent a long time, Folly said, "I suppose one good escape for Elise would be a marriage."

Stenfax flinched at the idea. "She isn't to be out of mourning for another few months. And that scene at the ball would likely make it difficult."

"It may be part of why Ambrose created it," Marina said with a frown. "If Elise is resistant to his advances, he is the kind of man who would work to eliminate any hope for her to

97

escape."

Stenfax got to his feet. The more he heard, the more concerned he was for Elise's safety in this volatile situation. And the more he realized just why she was pursuing a protector. Scandal surrounding her wouldn't matter to a man who only wanted her as a lover. And with the right man she would find a home, money for herself and true protection from the new duke's twisted desires.

But she had to find that protector soon, it seemed.

"You are very involved in this for a man who claims to have no connection to the duchess," Folly said.

Stenfax frowned as he looked at his friends. "I never said I had no connection. We all know that isn't true. I just hope I can ask you not to speak to Gray about this conversation. You know how he worries."

Marina laughed. "If you don't think Gray isn't already worried, you're a fool, my dear. He is convinced you may be caught in Elise's web a second time. Only Rosalinde has kept him from locking you up in a cage and shipping you back to the country already."

"Thank God for Rosalinde," Stenfax muttered. "But please, I promise you both, I will not get myself hurt again. I just…I just want to make sure she won't either."

Marina tilted her head, and for a moment she had the strangest expression on her face. Then she said, "Are you certain you can perform both those feats at once?"

In truth, he wasn't. But he had to try. To protect Elise, he *had* to try.

Elise wrote a line in her letter and sighed. This activity should not have taken the last hour, but she was dreadfully distracted and unable to focus.

She knew exactly why she was distracted. Lucien. She had

been utterly miserable in the three days since they'd last been together. She'd wept, she'd stayed in her bed. The mourning she'd been pretending to feel for Toby was easily achieved at the thought of truly never seeing Lucien again.

She'd lost him once before, but this time seemed...*worse*.

She hadn't even been able to drag herself to Vivien's. Which was a very bad thing. Ambrose had written her once during the past three days. He was pushing her to either get in his bed or get out to the street.

So she was running out of time. But how could she surrender herself to a lover when everything hurt so much? Would she simply pretend any man in her bed was the man she really wanted there? Would she become one of those mistresses with the empty eyes who laughed while her soul was eaten from the inside out?

"There isn't any choice," she murmured, pushing her letter away and covering her eyes with her hand.

"Your Grace, I'm sorry to disturb."

She turned to find her butler, Wiggins, standing at the parlor door. His lined face was pulled down in a deep frown and she caught her breath.

"If my visitor is Ambrose, tell him I have a headache. Tell him I'm dead for all I care, I don't want to see him," she said, harsher than she should have.

"It's not the new duke," came a voice behind Wiggins, and Elise stiffened. She pushed to her feet when the owner of the voice forced his way past her servant and entered the room without invitation.

"Gray," she whispered.

"Your Grace?" the butler queried, shooting Gray a long look.

"It's fine. Leave us."

He did so, and she drew a long breath as she stared. Stenfax's younger brother, Grayson Danford, had once been a great friend of hers. She'd spent many days as a girl playing with Felicity, Gray, Stenfax and the son of one of their servants,

Asher. She remembered Gray's wide grin and his bright, mischievous eyes.

Today he looked at her like she was trash that had been deposited in his path, and her heart hurt.

"May I get you tea?" she asked.

He shook his head without speaking and she pressed her lips together. He wasn't going to make this easy. "I heard of your marriage late last year," she said, forcing her voice to be bright. "And I saw you with the lady when I was at the Swinton ball last week. She is lovely, Gray. And rumor says you are very happy, so I am happy for you."

Gray's face didn't soften even a fraction. "I'm not here to discuss Rosalinde," he said, his tone clipped. "This is not a social call, so you may drop the pretense. We both know we are not friends."

"We were once," she said, hoping her pain wasn't utterly obvious. It felt like it was slashed across her skin in that moment.

Gray barked out a laugh, and it was harsh. "That was before you broke Stenfax's heart. And Felicity's."

Elise caught her breath. What he said was fair, especially given what he knew of the circumstances. But oh, how it burned inside of her. She hated that she'd hurt both her best friend and the man she loved with all her heart.

She moved toward him, a hand lifted in a sign of surrender. "It isn't so simple," she explained. "It's far more complicated."

He shook his head slowly. "Do you think I give a damn about any lie you'd tell to save yourself?"

"Save myself?" she murmured. "What do you mean?"

Gray's dark eyes narrowed. "You think I don't know what you're doing, Your Grace?"

She blinked. "What am I doing?"

"Very well, if you want to make me say it. I know that you are looking for a protector," he said. When her eyes went wide, he said, "Oh, don't worry, no one is speaking of it in Society, at least not yet. But I have my ways of finding out."

She straightened her shoulders despite the deep humiliation

that made her limbs feel heavy and almost numb. "Do you intend to threaten me with that knowledge, because as you say, no one is speaking about it *yet*. But we both know my position in Society is so precarious that nothing you say or do will change it now."

His brow wrinkled. "This is not a threat, Your Grace. I am not the kind of man who would blackmail you."

She stared at him a long moment and remembered his kindness as a boy. She shook her head. "No, I know you are not. Then what *do* you come here for?"

"Your situation *must* be precarious if you would go to such desperate measures," he continued. "You turned to Stenfax from that desperation, did you not? Perhaps you hope he will marry you out of the danger you're in. Or at the very least, make you his mistress so that you can escape."

"That isn't true!" Elise burst out. "I didn't orchestrate anything between Stenfax and me."

Gray rolled his eyes. "Oh yes, I believe you, the ultimate liar and actress. You forget that I know what you are capable of doing to obtain whatever you desire."

She turned away. She was so low in his estimation that nothing she said would be believable to him. And what was worse was that Stenfax felt the same way. He was not so hard as Gray, but he had said he couldn't trust her.

There was nothing she could do or say or explain to change any of their minds. This family that she had loved and longed to be a part of was lost to her. And she grieved that loss all over again, just as she had three years before when she'd turned away from it the first time.

"So you came here to call me a mercenary and a whore," she said softly. "Now that you have done so, are you finished, Gray?"

"Not quite. I came here to tell you to stay away from my brother."

She spun to face him, surprised by those words. Stenfax and Gray were best friends as well as brothers. Obviously Gray knew of their affair, but in three days Stenfax apparently hadn't told him about ending the affair. Why?

"I don't care about your desperation, I don't care about your lies, I don't care about *anything* except that you stay away from Stenfax," Gray continued, his gaze cold and even.

She swallowed hard. "You are too late in your order, Gray. Stenfax has already ended things with me. He hasn't seen or talked to me in days. I have no doubt he will never come to see me again. And if you're worried about me, I will not pursue him. I'm perfectly aware of the damage I did before. Of the damage I could do if...well, it doesn't matter. It's over. And my word will have to appease you, for I have no other proof excerpt for it."

Gray held her stare for a long moment and there was a strange expression on his face as he did so. As if he had searched for her lies and instead found a kernel of truth. He finally nodded swiftly.

"See that it *is* over. Good day." He turned away and stalked from the room without so much as a backward glance for her.

Once he was gone, Elise sank into a chair, her hands shaking, though Gray certainly hadn't posed any threat. But still, his appearance moved her.

Because it reminded her of the stakes. She couldn't spend time mourning the loss of her love. She couldn't regather herself.

No, she had to go to Vivien's tonight. She *had* to find a protector. That was the only way to end this.

Once and for all.

CHAPTER TWELVE

Lucien sat in a dark corner of Vivien's club, watching Elise across the room. He had arrived before her and she didn't know he was here as she stood with a small group of men, smiling and laughing with them. She was utterly beautiful in a low-cut blue gown, her hair in a loose chignon with curls that framed her face perfectly.

She didn't look lost like he was. She didn't look broken. So once again, he was the one shattered by their parting. She could just move on.

He frowned at the thought, even though he knew exactly why she was with those other men. He knew the threat she faced. He was here to help ensure she was protected, after all.

Vivien slipped into a chair beside him and smiled. "Hello, my lord."

"Vivien," he said, not in the mood to share his night with anyone, but especially the observant courtesan.

"I never pegged you for a voyeur," she said, leaning over so she could follow his line of sight. "Or perhaps it is only one lady who inspires such...proclivities."

He kept his lips pressed together, not rising to her bait as he kept watching Elise. She was with a middle-aged man named Carter and the much older Earl of Ryland.

But the companion who bothered him most was the young buck Winstead, who had approached her at the Swinton party the previous week. He was an eager sort, clearly interested in having her, if his long looks at her bosom were any indication.

She spent more time talking to him than the other two.

"Have you ever asked her why she threw you over?" Vivien asked, like a fly buzzing in his ear.

He jerked his face toward Vivien. "Most people don't dare to broach that subject with me," he said through clenched teeth.

Vivien didn't seem to be moved. "I'm not most people. Have you?"

He looked at Elise again. The other two men had drifted away now. It was just her and Winstead. The young man touched her arm and he thought he saw Elise stiffen slightly before she smiled.

"No," he said in answer to Vivien's question. Also as a response to Elise's slow surrender to another man.

"You're afraid of the answer."

He looked at Vivien again. Her words were correct, in a way. He kept telling Elise he didn't trust her, but it was more than that. He didn't want her to say those things out loud. To verify what had haunted him for years.

"I already know the answer," he said. "My father and grandfather and his father before him, they were terrible managers and gamblers all. They pissed away the estate in tiny increments. Building it back is tasked to me and it is a slow process. Elise's duke had blunt and a higher title. Everything else she ever said to me was a lie."

Vivien was silent for a long moment, and then she leaned in. "Does it feel like a lie when you're with her?"

"No," he ground out. "But I can't trust her."

"You won't let yourself," Vivien corrected.

"That's right." Lucien pressed a fist against the tabletop. "I know how that story ends. I can't even trust myself. Not anymore."

He looked at Elise again. She and Winstead were dancing now. She smiled when she was looking at him, but when she wasn't, her face looked…sad.

He pushed to his feet. "I came here tonight not to talk to you about my past with Elise, but to make sure she had a future. I have heard nothing negative about Winstead."

"Nor have I," Vivien said. "He is young, but he has means."

Lucien nodded. "Well, then it seems she is making a future just fine. She doesn't need me. She never did."

Vivien watched him for a moment, a knowing expression on her face. Then she inclined her head. "You seem to be ready to go. Good evening, Stenfax."

"I won't be back. Goodbye, Vivien."

And he turned and fled the room before Elise saw him. Before he had to see her locked in a future that once again didn't include him.

Elise watched as Winstead shut the terrace door behind himself and stepped toward her with a smile. He was a handsome enough young man, but she felt nothing as he reached for her hand and drew her toward the terrace wall.

All she could think about was Lucien.

"May I call you Elise?" Winstead asked.

She nodded. "I would prefer it, truth be told."

He smiled. "And you shall call me Theo," he said.

She tried to keep her expression serene as he reached up to brush a lock of hair from her cheek. But in her mind, she saw Lucien again. Lucien doing the same a dozen times before and after she had betrayed him.

"I want to be your protector," Winstead said softly.

She caught her breath. This was what she had been waiting for, and yet she felt no pleasure in the pronouncement. "Yes?"

"I have been enchanted by you since I first saw you here, Elise. Would you be interested in my taking that role?"

She drew a long breath. *Interested* was not the best term for it. *Resigned to it* fit better, but there was no use in engaging in semantics. It wasn't this man's fault that he wasn't the one she loved or that circumstances had forced her to this path.

She forced a smile and said, "Yes. I would."

"Good, then we must come to terms," he said, his face lighting up. "I admit you are my first mistress."

She flinched at the reminder that this man was several years younger than she. "Well, you are my first protector, so we'll learn together."

He leaned, and his breath was warm on her lips. "So we shall."

He kissed her then. A warm, sensual kiss that should have curled her toes. Instead all she felt was horrible guilt. She was betraying Stenfax just like she had betrayed him once before. She was betraying *herself* and everything in her heart.

And yet she had nothing to do about it. When Winstead pulled away, he smiled. "I have been waiting to do that a while now. Thank you."

She nodded slowly. "Terms," she encouraged him.

"Ah, yes. Well, I have small home to provide you. And an allowance, which I think is generous enough to manage what you would like to have."

"I have a maid. May I bring her?" she asked.

"Of course. I will include her wages in the household expenses." Winstead leaned back and looked at her, his eyes filled with a hungry, eager light. "I'd like to call on you twice weekly if you'd be open to that. And we could go to an event together once a month or so."

He was being very reasonable in his requests and yet Elise's heart had begun to pound with anxiety. When he said he wished to call on her, he meant visit her to take her to bed. She would go to his bed. Hell, she was rather surprised he hadn't insisted they make love already as some kind of test.

"Elise?" he pressed, his face falling slightly at her silence.

"I'm sorry," she said. "I'm—I'm nervous, I admit. All of that seems fine, Theo. But may I ask that…that we make the move quickly? My situation at my current home is precarious and it would be better if I went sooner rather than later."

His eyes widened slightly. "I had no idea, I'm sorry.

Certainly, I can have you moved in a few days at most if that will work for you."

She breathed a sigh of relief. "Yes, very much so."

"Good." He leaned in and kissed her again. She tried with all her might to sink into it, but couldn't manage it. He didn't seem to notice. "Now I'd love to go into one of Vivien's rooms and seal the deal properly," he said, and she stiffened as he reached for her. "But I think I'd like to have you the first time in the home I provide for you. When I know you're mine."

She almost collapsed in relief. "Yes. That would be very nice," she said.

"Excellent. I'll have my man write up an agreement with terms and send it to your home tomorrow. Begin preparations for your move."

He caught her in his arms with a laugh and kissed her again, but as Elise clung to him, she fought tears. This was what she'd wanted, planned for, what she needed.

And yet she wasn't happy in the slightest. And she knew no matter how hard she tried, she never would be. And *that* was the ultimate punishment for her past.

"Your Grace?"

Elise jerked her face toward her maid, Ruth, and found the young woman staring at her with a strange expression.

"This is good news, isn't it?" Ruth asked.

Elise blinked. She had just told her charge about her arrangements with Winstead. "Yes," she said slowly. "There is just much to be arranged. And we must do it quietly so that the Duke of Kirkford doesn't get wind of it. I cannot imagine he'll be pleased with my decision."

She shivered at the thought of what Ambrose would do when he realized she'd taken a lover and it wasn't him.

Ruth frowned. "I'll pack as discreetly as possible."

Elise nodded. "Good."

She looked at herself in the mirror. Her hair was down and her night rail and robe were on. She looked ready for bed, but although she ached from exhaustion, she doubted she would get a wink.

"You—you don't *look* happy, Your Grace," Ruth whispered. "I'm sorry if that's forward."

"No," she said with a reassuring glance at her maid. "I-I just didn't think this is where my life would take me."

No, she'd had an entirely different future not so very long ago. With Stenfax. If she had married him when she was meant to, by now they would perhaps have a child. His beautiful child.

She bent her head and squeezed her eyes shut to keep the tears from falling. She couldn't surrender to this pain or it would swamp her, destroy her. She had to be strong because there was no other alternative.

Suddenly there was a great pounding at her door. She jerked her head up and leapt to her feet, facing the barrier. "Who is it?" she asked.

"Let me in, Elise, or I shall kick this bloody door down!"

She gasped. It was the drunken voice of Ambrose, himself, that came from the hall. She exchanged a look of utter terror with Ruth.

"What shall we do?" Ruth whispered.

Elise looked toward the dressing room. "Go out through the adjoining room door. I don't want him taking out his anger on you."

"But Your Grace—" Ruth began, eyes wide as saucers.

"Do it," she insisted, all but pushing her maid toward escape that she, herself, could not take.

The girl did as she'd been told, but shot one last fearful look over her shoulder as she departed. Elise smoothed her robe and said, "Ambrose, I'm unlocking the door. Stop!"

He did not, continuing to pound so hard that the hinges of the door shuddered with each smashing fist. She shook with terror as she moved to the door and turned the key.

The moment she did, he thrust it open, nearly running her down as he rushed inside the chamber. She backed away at rapid speed, looking briefly to the drawer of her dressing table. She had a gun in that drawer. She'd put it there years ago, to guard against her husband when he was in a similar mood to his cousin's.

Now she was glad she'd never removed it.

"What is it, Ambrose?" she asked.

He stared at her, his gaze sliding over her informal nightgown and hair around her shoulders. He let out a belch before he said, "What do you *think* I'm doing here?"

She drew in a few long breaths to remain calm. "I don't know, but you have no right to burst into my house, my chamber, in the middle of the night!"

He tilted his head. "*My* house, you grasping whore. And I'm here because I heard about your little trips to Vivien Manning's."

She froze. Vivien had assured her that Ambrose was not allowed to hold a membership in her club. And most didn't speak about what they saw or did there, out of fear they'd lose their own membership. But Elise had always known she was taking a chance going there, making public her desire to find a protector.

It seemed her chickens were now coming home to roost, if Ambrose's wild-eyed rage was any indication.

"I don't know what you're talking about. I've never even heard of this person," she said, trying to keep the quaver from her voice. Failing miserably.

"Don't lie to me!" he roared. "Someone saw you there and reported it back to me. If you want to spread your legs for anyone who offers blunt, then here."

He tossed her a shilling and it bounced off her chest and clattered to the floor. She supposed the small value of the coin was meant to be insulting, but she wasn't insulted. She was abjectly terrified.

"Now take off your clothes," he demanded, beginning to

109

strip off his jacket as he said it.

"No," she said, not daring to move.

He made a sound of rage so deep in his throat that she nearly collapsed in terror right there. Then he rushed at her, crossing the room in a few long steps. She braced herself, her mind turning back to a very long ago summer day when Gray, Asher and Stenfax had taught Felicity and her how to throw a punch.

She hardly recalled their teachings, but as Ambrose moved to grab her, she shot out a fist and hit him. She hadn't fully closed the fist, though, so her finger darted out and she clawed him in the eye.

He staggered back, covering his eye with his hand as he made a sound of pain. With his other hand, he swung and backhanded her across the left cheek so hard that she saw stars. The force of the blow sent her reeling into her dressing table. Her hip crashed into the wood and pain shot through her.

"Goddamn bitch! You will pay for that."

She didn't think anymore. Her body seemed to entirely function on its own volition. She yanked her drawer open. A small double-barreled flintlock pistol waited inside. She pulled it from its hiding place and pulled back the hammer as she spun back to level it on Ambrose's chest.

He stopped moving toward her, and for a moment the room was silent as they stared at each other.

"What a tiny little pistol you have there, Your Grace," he finally chuckled.

Her hands were shaking, but she didn't lower the weapon. "I was assured that it fires just as well as any larger version, Ambrose. If you'd like to test it, I'm happy to show you."

She wished her voice sounded more calm, more collected, but it trembled just as she trembled from head to toe.

"Put it down, Elise," he insisted.

She shook her head. "I shall not."

He scowled but didn't advance. "You think that if you stop me tonight, that you'll stop me forever? I'll just come back."

She bit her lip and decided to play her cards. "I won't be

here. I *did* go to Vivien's, just as you have heard. I've found a protector, Ambrose, and I'm leaving this place."

His face twisted in rage. "You think you can walk away?" he bellowed, his voice all but shaking the room.

"I know I can," she said. "And I don't want to spill your blood on the way out, but I *will* if you take one more step toward me."

"All right," he said softly, his demeanor and tone terrifyingly calm after all his rage and bluster. "You go. You go tonight, in fact, if you think you're so high and mighty. But know this. It's not over. I know about Toby's book."

She swallowed hard past the lump of pure terror in her throat and stared at him. "Book, what book?"

"Don't play stupid, Elise. You know what book," he said.

She drew back. "I don't know, Ambrose, and I don't care."

"You should," he said with a bark of laughter. "It's the book where he kept all the secrets he used against people. Including, I would wager, yours."

Cold terror settled over every part of her body, but she refused to react. "I have no secrets," she lied.

Ambrose cocked his head with an incredulous look. "He had to get you somehow."

"You know how he got me. A higher title and a bigger purse. That's all there is to it."

"I don't think so," Ambrose said with a smile. "Because all the world is talking about how you're bedding Stenfax again, too. And I saw you two on the terrace last week. The way you looked at him, you wouldn't have walked away unless my dearly departed cousin had something powerful on you." His smile grew wider. "Or maybe not on you. Maybe someone else you cared for."

She shook her head. "No," she whispered.

"Yes, I've heard enough of that tonight." Ambrose turned toward the door. "You're delaying the inevitable, Elise. You know that. I will have you, whether by force or by striking a bargain once I know what lies and secrets you hold in that icy heart of yours. Now you and your maid get out of my house. My generosity ends tonight."

He stepped into the hall, slamming the door behind him. Elise sank to her knees, the gun still lifted, staring at the place where he'd gone. The door to the dressing room opened and she turned the gun toward it, but it was Ruth who stepped through. The girl shrieked in horror when she came face to face with the gun.

"Oh, Your Grace," Ruth whispered as Elise lowered the weapon. "Your eye!"

Elise blinked. In her terror, she'd forgotten that Ambrose had struck her. Her eye immediately began to throb and she lifted a hand to find it swollen already.

She could hold back no longer. She bent her head, her body shaking, and the tears began to fall. Her maid edged toward her and knelt beside her, gently prying the gun from her aching fingers and setting it aside.

"I-I heard most of it," Ruth said.

Elise didn't respond, just kept crying. Tonight was the culmination of what felt like a lifetime of pain and disappointment. She had sacrificed her life, her future, for the secrets Toby had uncovered, but she'd truly believed they had died with the loathsome man.

Now it seemed they might not have. Everything she'd fought to protect was at risk again. Everything she had done could very well be for nothing.

"Where will we go?" the maid asked.

Elise lifted her head. That was a very good question. Winstead had offered to be her protector tonight, but she had no idea where he lived, nor if he would accept her if she appeared there.

And the fact was that the secrets Ambrose threatened had everything to do with Stenfax. She had tried very long to protect him, to protect his family, from those secrets coming out.

But now it seemed she was out of her depth. He had a right to know about the threat she couldn't adequately protect him from.

"We will go to the Earl of Stenfax," she whispered, wiping at her tears and pushing to her feet on shaky legs. "It is the only option now, no matter how I've tried to avoid it. Pack as much as you can as quickly as you can. We leave within the half hour."

CHAPTER THIRTEEN

Stenfax dug his fingers into Elise's hair, dragging her body against his as he kissed her deeply, passionately. She moved against him, whispering how she loved him over and over. But in the background, there was a persistent sound. *Bang, bang, bang.*

He tried to ignore it, tilting her face toward his, seeing all her love there, watching all the time and the lies bleed away until they could be together.

Bang, bang, bang.

And in that moment, he realized this was a dream.

"No!" he said, holding tighter, but she was fading, fading away.

He opened his eyes and sat up with a start. The banging at his chamber door was loud and constant.

"My lord? My lord?" It was his butler Xavier's voice in the hall.

"Come in, Xavier," Stenfax grunted, adjusting the covers over his naked body. "For Christ's sake, just stop knocking."

The door opened and Stenfax flinched at the light from the hall, raising his hand to block it and the shadow of his servant entering the darkened room.

"I'm sorry to disturb, my lord," Xavier said.

"What bloody time is it?" Stenfax grunted.

"After three, sir," Xavier said.

Stenfax looked at him. The normally impeccable butler was in his dressing gown and a crooked nightcap. He held a candle that gave his wrinkled face an eerie glow.

"Why are you in my room at three in the morning?" Stenfax asked, but he despite his calm tone, he was beginning to worry. There was no good reason he would be disturbed by his staff like this. Only tragic ones.

"You have a visitor, my lord," Xavier said, and from his shifting, he was very uncomfortable giving this news.

"Who?" Stenfax said, his tone sharp at last.

"It's the Duchess of Kirkford, my lord. And a maid." The man shifted again. "And a small valise."

"What?" Stenfax barked, throwing the covers off and grabbing for his robe.

"They—they arrived very suddenly and I put them in the parlor. They both seemed very upset and—" The servant cut himself off and Stenfax took a step toward him.

"And?"

"Her Grace has a nasty bruise on her eye, my lord."

Stenfax tensed. He had left Vivien's club hours before and Elise had been seemingly safe in the arms of Winstead. Now she was here and injured.

"She was hit," he ground out past clenched teeth.

"It appears so," Xavier said with a solemn nod.

Stenfax took a long breath, mostly so he wouldn't scream out his anger and anguish at her pain. Then he looked at Xavier. "Send the maid to the servants' quarters, make sure she's comfortable there. And the valise may be taken up to a chamber for her ladyship. You choose, and leave the door open so I may escort her there later. I'll be down in a moment to speak to Elise—Her Grace."

"Yes, sir." Xavier executed a sharp bow before he moved for the door.

"And Xavier?" Stenfax said, keeping him from departing.

"Yes?" the butler asked, turning back.

"The wine tonight was chilled. Do we still have any ice?"

"A little," Xavier said. "Most has melted."

"Gather what we have left in a cloth and give it to Her

Grace. For her injury."

Xavier nodded, and this time Stenfax let him leave the room. He paced the chamber for a moment, not because he didn't want to rush down to meet Elise, but because he desperately did want to. He needed to be calm before he saw her. Whatever she'd been through that night, he wasn't about to make it worse by panicking and blustering.

Except he wasn't going to be calm. He knew it. He also knew something else, powerfully and clearly. He was in love with Elise. Still. Always. Forever.

And it was awful.

Elise sat in the chair by the fire, waiting for Lucien, as she had been directed to do by his butler Xavier a few moments before. Ruth had gone with the servant, valise in hand, and Elise had been alone ever since.

Alone was not a good place to be in her current mindset. She kept reliving those terrifying moments with Ambrose, the stark realization that he would rape her, and after she hurt his eye, that he might even do worse than that.

She also kept reliving his threats. Could he be right that Toby had a book of secrets? She wouldn't put it past him. He'd loved to hold those kinds of things over people, for sport rather than gain. He had lived to control and hurt.

He had died doing the same, in a duel over a married woman who he hadn't even cared about. He'd just wanted to get one over on her husband.

Which had also been his motivation for "taking her" from Stenfax. She had been a trophy during their marriage, nothing else. He brought her out when he wanted to show her off and ignored her when he didn't.

She shivered at the cruelty of both the former Duke of Kirkford and the current. Luckily her thoughts were interrupted when Xavier returned to the parlor with a cloth in his hand.

"For your eye, Your Grace," he said, not meeting her gaze as he handed over the item.

She took it and felt the coldness of ice folded within the soft layers of fabric. She lifted it with a blush and covered her throbbing eye.

"Thank you," she whispered.

He nodded. "The earl will be with you momentarily. And your maid is very comfortably situated now, so you won't have to worry about her."

Elise managed a smile for the kindness of Stenfax's butler. She certainly did not deserve as much.

"Good night, Your Grace. If I can be of any service tomorrow, I hope you will not hesitate." He executed a swift bow then left her to herself again.

Elise sighed and rose to her feet, walking over to the fire to stare at it with the eye that wasn't currently covered. The other one still hurt, but the ice did help a bit.

"Elise?"

She turned and caught her breath. Stenfax stood in the doorway, a robe tied around his waist, but his legs and feet were bare and a V of naked chest was visible through the top of the dressing gown. He was not wearing anything beneath, and her body tensed despite everything she'd been through that night.

He said nothing else, just moved across the room toward her. She waited for him, motionless and wordless as he gently caught her hand and lowered the cloth from her eye.

His gaze went wide and his lips turned down in an angry scowl as he looked at her eye. She hadn't looked at it yet, but she could feel that it was swollen.

"Goddamn it," he said, and then lifted the ice back to cover the injury.

"It doesn't hurt," she whispered.

"Liar," he bit out, his tone harsh and hard.

She bent her head. Yes, they both knew she was that. But tonight had stripped all those lies away. All the truths would come out now. She might as well start practicing on easier ones than the ones to come.

"It does hurt," she admitted. "But it will fade."

"Better," he said. "Who did this to you? Winstead?"

She caught her breath as she looked at him again. "H-how did you know I was with Winstead tonight?"

He let out a long sigh. "I went to Vivien's. I-I saw you with him."

She pursed her lips. "Do you also know we agreed to terms tonight?"

He stiffened and his jaw twitched, answering her question before he bit out. "No. I did not."

"It wasn't him who did this, Lucien."

"Then who?" he asked, his voice still rough as he reached out to trace her jaw with his fingertips. "Who did this?"

She fought for calm. The truth had never been easy with this man. Even less so now that it was a Pandora's Box of pain waiting to be unleashed on both of them and everyone else they loved.

"The new Duke of Kirkford," she admitted softly.

Everything on Lucien's face went dark and hard. Like a storm on an angry sea, he looked utterly destructive and dangerous.

"He burst into my room, demanding—" She cut herself off with a sob she hadn't even known was coming. "But I didn't let him."

Silently, Lucien slid his arms around her and drew her against his chest. He smoothed a hand over her hair as he whispered, "You don't have to tell me tonight. There will be plenty of time to do it tomorrow. But I do want to ask one thing."

She nodded against his chest, soothed by his embrace, by his scent, by everything that she loved about him.

"If you came to terms with Winstead, why did you come here after you were attacked?"

She let out a broken breath. "Because I didn't know where he lived," she admitted, and felt Stenfax stiffen. She lifted her gaze so he could see her eyes. "And because I knew you would keep me safe. Even if I don't deserve it."

His expression softened and he whispered, "You don't *deserve* to be in danger, Elise. Now, come. It's very late and we can talk about everything tomorrow. Let me take you upstairs."

He took her hand and led her from the room, led her up the long staircase and down a hallway. A door there had been left open and he drew her through. She looked around.

It was a guest chamber, plain but serviceable. It was still cool in the room, which was to be expected considering she had just arrived and the servants who had been awakened to deal with her being there had only a few moments to ready it. Her valise rested on a table by the window and the covers had been drawn down on the bed.

It wasn't Lucien's room, of course. She had never seen Lucien's room. The night they stole—made love, before their engagement was destroyed—was in her old room in the home of her late parents. He'd snuck through her window.

She shook the memories away and looked at him. He was just…watching her, and had made no move to come farther into the room, nor to leave her.

"It's lovely," she whispered.

He shrugged. "It's safe for tonight. Safe until we can work this out."

She moved toward him a step, unable to stop herself. Unable to keep from lifting a hand to caress his cheek with her palm. He shut his eyes with a long exhalation and leaned into her touch.

"Will you stay?" she asked softly.

His eyes came open, dark and hooded as he stared down at her. But also resistant. And she knew why. They had stated this affair was at an end, if he took her one more time it muddled everything.

Tonight, though, taking wasn't the first thing on her mind. It wasn't the last, either, but it wasn't why she asked him to stay.

"I keep picturing him coming across the room at me," she

admitted with a catch to her breath. "So I ask you not so you'll make love to me, but just so you'll...stay."

He held her gaze for a long moment and she could tell he was analyzing her words for their veracity. Even in this, he didn't believe her. But why would he? She had earned no less.

He said nothing as he took her hand again and moved her toward the bed. He turned her and began unbuttoning the gown Ruth had hastily helped her into over her night rail. She held her breath as his big hands brushed gently over her skin, warming her, soothing her.

He pushed the dress away and looked at her. "You really did have to run, didn't you?" he murmured, staring at the thin night rail with its stitched straps.

She dipped her chin. "You think I punched myself in the eye just to manipulate you into saving me?"

He considered that a moment. "No. I don't. I'm sorry if I sounded like I doubted you. I don't. Now, come."

He motioned the bed and she got under the covers and slid over, leaving him a space. He shut his eyes, took a long breath, and when he opened them he started to get in beside her, his dressing gown still tied around his waist.

"You sleep in your robe?" she asked.

His gaze snagged hers. "I sleep in nothing. I didn't think that would be a particularly good idea, considering."

She licked her lips and his eyes went wide, but he got into the bed regardless and snuffed the candle on the side table.

"Roll over," he whispered in the dark. "Face the window."

She did, putting her back to him, and he tucked himself around her from behind, drawing her back against his warm chest. One hand rested on her stomach, the other supporting her neck beneath the pillow.

She settled back against him, burrowing into his embrace. Oh yes, she could feel the stiffness of his cock against her backside. He wanted her. She wanted him. But for now, that wasn't the reason he was here.

He was here to protect her, to comfort her, and that meant

more than any passion they might share. For the first time in years, her body relaxed, welcoming sleep rather than fearing it. And she drifted off with Lucien's breath warm on her neck and his body cradling hers.

Lucien opened one eye slowly. He hadn't shut the inside curtains last night, so it was only the flimsy ones meant for privacy that covered the window. Morning sunshine flowed into the room, cascading over the bed and the woman beside him.

At some point she had rolled onto her back, and so he had the perfect view of her relaxed face, her full lips and the nasty black eye that even the ice hadn't kept from swelling and darkening.

His stomach clenched at the sight of her damaged. He would kill that son of a bitch for touching her. For trying to do worse than just blacken her eye.

Her gaze fluttered open, her gaze bleary with sleep, and she whispered, "This is always my favorite dream."

She lifted a hand to cup the back of his head and drew him down, lifting her lips to his. He should have pulled back, resisted, but he couldn't. He kissed her back, gently, but gentle didn't matter. His body was already hard and touching her made it worse, not better.

She moved against him with a sleepy murmur, and then she pulled back suddenly and stared up at him. He could see her realizing that this wasn't whatever dream she referenced. He was really there. She was really there. That was really his cock pushing into her stomach.

Her breath was short, her pupils dilated as she reached between them and pushed the folds of his robe aside. She found his cock and took him in hand, sliding her fingers down the length gently.

"Damn it, Elise," he murmured as he pressed his mouth

against her neck. He sucked there as she stroked, precariously perched on the edge of losing all control.

But he didn't. Slowly, she rolled until she was on top of him, straddling his lap, lowering her mouth to his. He sucked at her tongue, desperate to be joined with her, and she shuddered in pleasure. Her hand reached between them, she guided him into position and suddenly he was sliding into wet, tight heat. She rippled around him, pulsing and massaging as she let out a broken, heated moan of pleasure.

She shifted her hips, lifting against him, rubbing him, and he was utterly lost in sensation. She moved with purpose, driving toward her pleasure and dragging him along for the ride. It didn't take long for her to find it. She let out a soft cry that she muffled by kissing him, and her hips pumped hard against him. He knew he was going to come, he couldn't stop it, and he pulsed up hard into her, finding his pleasure without withdrawing from her heat.

She pulled away, her breath short, and they stared at each other, recognizing what they'd just done. What could come out of it.

She rolled away and sat up. "I didn't manipulate that," she said.

He stared at her. She felt she had to defend herself, and why wouldn't she? He'd been accusing her of much worse behavior and manipulations for weeks now. But looking at her, thinking about what they'd just done, he realized he felt no such accusation toward her now.

"No, I don't think you did. I could have moved you."

She pushed to her feet and her nightgown fell around her hips and legs. She paced toward the window, the light framing her like an angel. "I would *never* trap you."

He got up too, watching the emotions play on her face. Was she upset because he might have ruined her plans to find a lover to protect her? Or was it really that she didn't want to be judged by him, hated by him?

In the end, he supposed it didn't matter.

"I'll ring for your maid," he said softly. "Get dressed and

join me for breakfast. There is a great deal for us to discuss."

She turned on him, and now her look went from concern to abject terror. Slowly she nodded. "Yes. I have so much to tell you, Lucien. So much to say."

He backed up a step, uncertain how to proceed when she had such an expression. In the end, he just nodded. "I'll see you downstairs."

He moved to the door, ringing the bell for her servant as he walked out. But in the hallway, he leaned against the wall, catching his breath. He'd spent his life looking backward and identifying moments when everything had changed. When his father died and he became earl, when Elise left him and destroyed everything and now...*this* moment. In his heart he knew everything was about to change.

He just didn't know how. And that terrified him.

CHAPTER FOURTEEN

Lucien stood in the breakfast room nearly an hour later, dressed and pressed and looking every inch the Earl of Stenfax. But he felt less than impeccable as he poured himself a cup of tea and looked idly toward the door. In a few moments Elise would walk through and then...

Well, he still couldn't shake the feeling that everything was about to change.

"Good morning, my lord," Xavier said as he came to the entry of the breakfast room.

Lucien let out a breath he hadn't known he was holding and nodded. "Xavier. Thank you again for your help last night. Her Grace will be joining me for breakfast shortly, and if you are wondering about future arrangements, I honestly have none to share with you until I speak to her."

"I understand, sir. The truth is, I came to tell you that your family is here."

Lucien slowly set his cup back on the saucer. "My family?"

"Mr. and Mrs. Danford and Lady Barbridge," the butler clarified. "Your mother does not seem to be in attendance."

Lucien sighed deeply, for he almost wished his mother *were* here. Lady Stenfax would still Felicity's and Gray's tongue in a way Rosalinde could not.

Especially since there would be no hiding that Elise was here. Nor that her eye was blackened. Nor anything else.

"Any chance they might be persuaded that I'm not in residence?" he asked, knowing the answer even before Xavier shifted in discomfort.

"Mr. Danford said if you asked me that I was to tell you, 'we're not leaving so you might as well stop hiding'. I do apologize, my lord, I'm just the messenger."

"Of course you are, I don't blame you. Just send them in." Lucien straightened his waistcoat and remained standing. Within a moment, Gray, Rosalinde and Felicity all came through the door.

"Good morning," Lucien forced through a tight jaw. "I don't recall you sending word you would be calling. I'm afraid it's a bit inconvenient to receive you this morning."

Rosalinde at least had the decency to look chagrined at that remark, but Felicity and Gray did not. Gray, in fact, folded his arms and grunted, "I don't care about the inconvenience, Stenfax. We need to speak to you."

Felicity shot their brother a look and moved toward Lucien with a much gentler air. "Lucien, we are all worried."

"And I appreciate it. But I must tell you that Elise—"

She caught his arm. "Elise is exactly the topic we've come here to broach. Please, won't you let us speak without interruption, without argument?"

He pressed his lips together. He was trying to warn them of Elise's being there and all of them were determined to perform some kind of...mediation with him on that very subject.

"I'm trying to tell you—"

"We all know you've been bedding her," Gray interrupted.

Rosalinde blushed and shot Lucien an apologetic look before she said, "I thought we weren't going to be so blunt, my love."

Gray shook his head. "I'm sorry, Rosalinde. This is too important a matter to dance around. Lucien, I had hoped that your obsession with the woman would pass, but I fear it isn't, so I must tell you that I worry about what happened before."

Felicity was nodding along with him, and Lucien stiffened. "There is no reason to discuss that," he snapped. "The subject is closed."

Gray threw up his hands in frustration and all but shouted, "Lucien, you once stood on a terrace wall and nearly threw yourself to your death because of this woman. How can I stand by idly while you tangle yourself in her web again?"

"Lucien?"

All four of them turned as a group and Lucien caught his breath. Elise was standing at the entrance to the breakfast room, her hands trembling at her sides, her face pale.

And he knew, without a doubt, that she had just overheard his brother's words. All of them.

Elise stared at Lucien, Gray's words ringing in her ears. Gray and Felicity were watching her—she felt their shocked gazes as they realized she was here and probably had been here since last night.

But she didn't care. All she cared about was Lucien.

"You almost killed yourself," she whispered. "Over—over me?"

His cheek twitched. She knew that motion all too well. It had always been a telltale sign of a subject he didn't like. One he didn't want to talk about.

He didn't move toward her, but he said, "I was very drunk, Elise. It was the night you threw me over and wouldn't see me."

She staggered back, nearly depositing herself on the floor as she lifted a hand to cover her trembling lips. Pain and guilt tore through her, like a bullet, like a knife, and she felt the tears beginning to stream down her face.

"Oh, Lucien, Lucien," she whispered.

Gray stepped between them at last and glared at her. She turned her face, unable to fully look at him when he was filled with such abject hatred for her. "You pretend to give a damn about his reaction when you wouldn't even see him? When you *had* to have known the damage you would do?"

"Stop," Lucien said, catching his brother's arm. Gray shook him off.

"No." Gray turned that same glare on his brother. "Someone needs to bloody well say it to her. You destroyed my brother, you hurt my sister, and now you want to flounce back into his life and pretend like you didn't?"

"I haven't pretended," Elise whispered, holding herself upright by gripping the back of the closest chair. "I have never forgiven myself for what I did to him and I shall *never* forgive myself now that I know what nearly happened because of me."

Felicity moved on her now as Gray spun away with a disgusted snort. Elise couldn't help but stare at her. She hadn't seen her best friend in three years. They had avoided each other just as Lucien had avoided her during that time. Now her mind spun back to girlish giggles and happy times.

Felicity looked beautiful, as she always had, even though her blonde hair was pulled back rather severely and she had nothing but contempt in her pale blue eyes.

"Don't you dare cry," Felicity whispered. Then she drew back and stared. "What—what is…your eye is black, Elise."

Elise turned away as Gray took a long step back toward her and his wife, Rosalinde, yanked a hand up to her mouth with a gasp. She had hoped, in their upset, they would all overlook that fact. Especially Felicity. Felicity, who had endured intense physical abuse at the hands of her late husband.

Felicity, who would suffer the most when the truth about Elise's lies came out.

"It's nothing," she said. "I *know* it's nothing. I don't want your pity."

But the tone of the room had softened with Felicity's observation and her friend backed away, less accusation in her stare.

Elise looked at Lucien again and he nodded slowly, as if encouraging her to say something, do something, brave something. And she had to now. There was no choice left. It was fitting that there would be an audience, *this* audience for what was to come.

"I came here last night, because the new Duke of Kirkford attacked me," she explained softly. "I had nowhere else to go—Ambrose has made certain of that. I *shouldn't* have turned to Stenfax. I deserve none of his kindness, nor anyone's understanding. I know that." She cleared her throat and turned away. "Under normal circumstances, I would simply walk away. I realized that would be better for *you*." She looked at Stenfax again. "But...I can't."

"Why?" Gray ground out. "Why do you claim you can't stop this madness?"

She shook her head. "Because something from the past has reared its ugly head. Something I thought I...I had managed. I was a fool to think I had. And I must tell you the truth." She let her gaze stray to Stenfax and found him staring back at her, even and almost *ready*. Like he knew something terrible was about to come and he braced for it. He didn't know the half of it. "I must tell you everything."

Gray's new wife stepped forward then, a gentle look on her face. Elise almost wept to see it, for it was the only kindness in this room full of anger and misunderstanding and apprehension.

"May I make a suggestion?" Rosalinde said softly. When no one answered, she plowed ahead anyway. "Why don't we go into the adjoining parlor and sit? This is obviously a highly emotional moment for everyone and it might make it easier, yes?"

"A fine idea," Stenfax croaked.

Rosalinde moved toward Felicity, who was still staring in disbelief and pain at Elise's black eye. She took her elbow and gently guided her from the room.

Stenfax shot Elise a look and she thought he might move to her, but Gray stepped in beside him instead and the two men left the room with her trailing behind them, outside their circle. Once she was done, she would never be let in again.

But then, she hadn't expected to be. Whatever she'd shard with Stenfax this past little while had been stolen from the start.

She'd never expected it to last, only hoped it would. And that had been her own foolish doing if she was now disappointed.

They entered the parlor off the breakfast room and Rosalinde situated everyone. She and Gray sat on the settee, her hand placed firmly over his. Felicity sat in one chair while Elise sank into another. But Stenfax did not sit.

No, he remained standing at the fireplace, his eyes locked on her.

"Begin," he said.

Elise drew in a long breath and kept her gaze on him. "I hardly know where to begin," she whispered.

"Why don't you start with the night you decided Lucien wasn't good enough for you," Felicity snapped.

Elise flinched and shot her former best friend a look. "I-I would start there, but that isn't the start of the story. The story starts not with Lucien and me, but with my late husband."

Lucien folded his arms. "Kirkford."

She nodded. "Yes, Kirkford. He had always hated you, Lucien. Gray, too, but mostly you. I heard about it for years after, though I didn't know it then. Do you know *why* he hated you?"

Lucien wrinkled his brow as he stared at her. "I have no idea. We were in school together and I though he was an ass, honestly."

"He *was* an ass," Gray muttered. "Don't know what that bloody well has to do with this."

"Let the poor woman speak," Rosalinde said softly. "I'm sure it will all become clear."

Elise gave Rosalinde a look of gratitude before she continued, "Yes, he hated you in school. He said you were 'golden'. No matter what, you always were popular, always were liked, where he...struggled."

"So he hated me because I had more friends in school. I don't really give a damn," Lucien said, his frustration clear.

She held up a hand. "That *isn't* why he hated you. Well, it *is*, but it isn't why he wanted to destroy you. About three and a half years ago, you were in a club, gambling at a table with him.

He was drinking and, apparently, cheating. You caught him."

Lucien looked confused for a moment, and then his face brightened with recollection. "Yes, I do remember that. He was drunk off his head and blustering. He'd just become duke, I think, and wanted to be treated as royalty. When I realized he was cheating, I called him out on it. He flipped a table and threw a punch—"

"And got publicly and permanently banned from the club," Elise finished for him, holding his gaze evenly.

Lucien drew back a little and nodded. "Yes, that part happened too."

"Well, it humiliated him. As you said, he had just become duke and he felt he deserved to be respected and revered. Everyone knew of your...financial situation, and yet you were still accepted. Liked. It was a final stray for Kirkford."

"The final straw," Gray said. "What does that mean?"

Elise turned toward Gray. "He decided he was going to destroy Lucien. And *that* is where the story begins to involve me."

Felicity pushed to her feet. "So you actively participated in this revenge by leaving my brother."

"No!" Elise snapped, spinning toward her. "Great God, you would think you knew me better after everything we went through, Felicity."

"I don't know you. I thought I did, but I never did," Felicity said back, her tone cold and dismissive.

Elise flinched away from it. "Sit down, I'll explain it now if everyone would stop interrupting me."

Felicity slowly did so, but she folded her arms and glared at Elise. Her contempt was vast and not masked in the slightest. It felt as painful as Ambrose's punch the night before.

Elise drew a long breath. Stenfax was staring at her now, no longer leaning on the fireplace mantel, but his body coiled with tension, like he was preparing for an attack.

"Kirkford came to me the night before I threw you over," she explained. "It was the night of some ball and I'd cried off with a headache, but my parents had gone. I was alone when he called. I hardly knew the man, but I was..." She sucked in a breath. "...*afraid*. There was something wrong with him and I recognized it right away. He told me that I would not be marrying you. He said within twenty-four hours I'd end my engagement."

Lucien moved forward. "And what made you go along with that?"

Now Elise faced Felicity again and shook her head. "I'm sorry, Felicity," she bit out. "I'm so sorry. He—he knew."

Felicity stiffened, going ramrod straight in the chair. "Knew?" she whispered.

"He knew," Elise repeated.

She recognized the moment Felicity fully understood her cryptic words. Her friend jumped up, backing away, her hands up, as if she could ward it off.

"What is she talking about?" Gray asked, looking at Felicity, then Elise, then Lucien.

"What *are* you talking about?" Lucien repeated, but only directed the question at Elise.

Elise ignored him for the time being. "I'm sorry," she repeated to Felicity.

"How? How?" Felicity asked, hitting the wall beside the door and flattening there, her hands shaking and all the color gone from her face.

"A servant, I think. He had a letter, signed by the man, confessing his part in it all. I wouldn't have believed it, but—but I'd seen you after and I'd always known something was wrong about the story you told. I should have pushed harder, I should have made you tell me. I should have been a better friend."

Lucien moved across the room in three long steps and placed himself between Elise and Felicity. He looked angry, but more than that, he looked apprehensive.

"Stop these riddles," he insisted, his voice suddenly too loud in the quiet room. "You say Kirkford knew something and that it was about Felicity. What is it he knew?"

Elise moved past him, reaching out to her former friend. And to her surprise, Felicity allowed her to take her hand. She clung to Elise like she was a lifeline.

"Should I say it?" Elise asked, blinking at tears.

Felicity shook her head. "No. It's my secret. I-I should tell them. I probably should have told them a long time ago."

Elise nodded slowly, then let Felicity go as she paced past her brother and took the spot where he'd been brooding by the fireplace. Elise moved forward and placed herself beside Lucien, resting a hand on his forearm in order to the give the support she knew he'd need in a moment.

"You all know what I endured at the hands of my husband," Felicity began, her voice trembling.

Both Gray and Lucien flinched, and Elise felt for them. When they'd realized Felicity was being abused by her bastard of a husband, both had tried to save her. But the man had been rich and powerful and Felicity's husband. The law recognized his right to *discipline* her as he saw fit. There had been no saving her, and both men had suffered greatly in their powerlessness.

"You know it was bad, but not how bad," Felicity continued, and now she was shaking all over. "By the end, his violence had escalated and I truly feared for my life. One night he came to my bedroom, demanding—" She broke off and gave Elise a look. "May I assume he was demanding the same thing the new Duke of Kirkford demanded of you?"

Elise nodded once. "Yes."

"When I wasn't as exuberant about the prospect as he'd like, he began to hurt me." Felicity's eyes brightened with tears that streamed down her cheeks. "And then he told me he was going to kill me. He was choking me, the life was leaving me. I hit him with a vase and he let me go, but he kept coming at me. So I grabbed the pistol from his waist and I shot him."

CHAPTER FIFTEEN

There was a collective gasp from everyone in the room at Felicity's confession. Lucien stared at his baby sister, whom he loved with all his heart, and couldn't stop shaking. Elise's hand tightened on his arm, holding him steady as he lived through the images of all Felicity had suffered, all she had kept silent over the years since that night.

"You killed him," Rosalinde finally whispered when the room had been silent for what seemed like an eternity and Felicity had not yet found the power to go on.

"Yes," Felicity said, the sound drawn out in a long whisper of brokenness and pain that felt like it pushed Lucien's own pain wider and fuller. "He died on the floor of my chamber, cursing my name. His family was powerful and as vindictive as he was, and I knew I would be arrested for the crime. No one would have cared that I'd defended my life—they would only care that I had killed a viscount. I was ready to call for the guard and face the consequences, but my husband's servants came to my rescue. They rallied around me, they made his death look like the hunting accident it was eventually claimed to be and they swore they would never tell the truth."

"But someone did," Elise whispered. "Someone did."

"That is what I've lived in fear about for years," Felicity sobbed. "And now to hear it's true..."

She buckled, and both Gray and Lucien rushed at her, catching her and both holding her as the three of them huddled together. Lucien had always respected Felicity's strength of character, her calm collectedness in the face of any situation. Now that was gone and she wept against Gray's shoulder, great wracking sobs that shook her slender frame violently. Lucien could do nothing except smooth her hair and whisper gentle words of comfort that felt so damned empty.

For not the first time, he longed to spin the clock backward and do anything in his power to stop Felicity from marrying the brute who had brought this on his family. But he couldn't.

"Felicity," Gray whispered as their sister's crying ceased. "Sweetest love, why didn't you tell us?"

She pulled back and looked first Gray, then Lucien, in the face. "Both of you already carried such guilt that you'd allowed the match, I couldn't allow you even more of it. And what could you have done? Barbridge was dead, the covering up of his murder complete. I saw no point in bringing up my secret and forcing you both to carry it with me."

Lucien felt no satisfaction in that answer and Gray didn't seem to either, judging from his pained expression. But Felicity didn't allow them time to respond. She pushed from the circle of their arms and moved toward Elise.

Stenfax turned toward her, too and was surprised to find that Rosalinde had silently joined her and had an arm around her as they watched the family process this bitter news. He found he was happy to see she had support when he couldn't provide it. After all, her part in this story wasn't over.

There was more to come and he dreaded it because he now had a clearer vision of what Elise had done and why. She would have to say it and he would have to hear it.

"*You* carried it with me," Felicity whispered, moving toward Elise. "This secret."

Elise swallowed hard, and it seemed she was bracing herself for a rejection from Felicity. She nodded. "I did."

"He told you about what he knew. I assume that was his way to destroy Lucien."

Elise drew a long breath. "He would have settled for that, of course. But he would have had to be very careful how he revealed your secret. Society could have eaten him alive if they found out he had such terrible information and turned it against you. You both might have burned in those flames. And even if he hadn't that concern, he wanted a more direct hit on Lucien. He wanted Lucien to know it was Kirkford who had bested him. So he offered me a choice."

She stopped, dipping her head. Her shoulders shook, her hands shook. Lucien couldn't see her like that. Not now.

"Throw me over and marry him or let him unleash the truth about Felicity into the world," he said softly.

Elise jerked her face up and met his gaze. Her green eyes were bright with pain and regret and loss. "Yes," she admitted. "*That* was his bargain. Hurt you by rejecting you as I did, orchestrated by him. Or allow your entire family to be destroyed in a flurry of trial, prison, death and destruction."

Stenfax reeled away as the full weight of this confession crushed him like a vise around his heart. He pictured that night long ago when he'd received her note ending their relationship, but now he knew she was being forced to write it. He thought of how he'd banged on her door and been refused, but now he knew she'd been upstairs brokenhearted about that choice.

He pictured all the times he'd hated her without knowing the truth. He'd thought his life was empty while she moved on, but in truth she had been just as desolate as he had. Only he'd had his family to support him. Her parents had died just after her marriage and she'd been left alone with a man who was capable of such twisted manipulation and cruelty.

"You chose the marriage," Felicity whispered, breaking through his tangled thoughts and making him look back at Elise. "Even though you knew it would be miserable."

"To protect you and Stenfax? Yes." Elise let out a long, shaky sigh, as if holding those words in for so long had been painful. "And I would have kept that secret, I would kept *your* secret, Felicity, until the day I drew my last breath. I would have endured your hatred and your censure with the knowledge that I'd done the best I could to protect you. Only now something has happened that forced my hand."

"What?" Gray asked, but for the first time his voice was not harsh toward her.

"After Ambrose attacked me, I drew a gun on him, just as you did on Barbridge." Stenfax caught his breath. He knew she'd been assaulted, but not how bad it had actually been. "It stayed his attack, thank God, but not his tongue. He vowed that he would have what he wanted one way or another. And he claimed..."

She covered her mouth as if what she would say was too painful. Felicity moved toward her, taking her hand. "What did he say?"

"Ambrose said that Toby, Kirkford the last, kept a book of all the secrets he held over others. A bragging book, I suppose you would call it. And though Ambrose has no idea of what could be in that book, if it exists and he finds it, I don't think he'd make a bargain for it. I think he would unleash the truth just to cause pain to me and to those I love."

Felicity released her hand and staggered across the room, back to the chair where she had started. She sat down in it with a hard thud and placed a hand over her eyes.

Stenfax stared at Elise, trying to remain calm, trying to get all the information before he reacted. "And do you think this book exists, or is the new Kirkford just toying with you?"

She thought for a moment before she nodded, almost apologetically, like she wished she could make this not true. He supposed she wished she could, after everything she'd been through to keep this secret at bay.

"It is very possible it exists," she admitted. "My late husband made attacks on *many* people during our years together."

Gray nodded. "Yes, there were always whispers of him and his behavior."

Elise sighed. "He enjoyed recounting his 'wins' as much as he enjoyed orchestrating them. I have little doubt he was capable of keeping such a diary for his own pleasure. A place to gather all his evidence, to review his misdeeds."

Stenfax bent his head. Well, there it was. A threat against his family unlike any they had ever faced. A fight they might not be able to win.

But even as that tore at him, he looked up at Elise and even more emotions stirred in his chest. So many he could barely name them. His brother and Rosalinde looked numb at the news, Felicity looked numb.

Stenfax was not numb. For the first time in the three years they'd been apart, every part of him was entirely aware, sharp, focused.

"There is obviously a great deal to discuss now," he said, his voice rough. "So much to discuss and plan and prepare for. But I need a moment alone with Elise."

She caught her breath at the statement, but didn't move from her spot across the room.

Slowly Felicity rose and smoothed her skirts. She seemed to have regained some of her composure, for her voice was steady as she said, "Of course."

Gray and Rosalinde moved toward the door, as well, but when Gray passed Elise, he stopped. They stared at each other for a moment, then he leaned in and pressed a kiss to her cheek. "Thank you," he murmured. "I don't know what else to say."

Elise wiped at tears. "There is nothing else to say."

He nodded swiftly and then the three of them left the room. Stenfax followed, shutting the door behind them. He turned and leaned against the barrier, staring at Elise as she remained just where she stood, her expression unreadable.

"How could you?" he whispered when he wanted to scream. "How could you not come to me when all this happened?"

She let out a long sigh. "What would you have done had I come to you? What would Gray have done?"

He slammed a hand back against the door and she jumped at the loud sound that did nothing to release the tension in his chest. "We would have confronted that bastard. We would have found a way to stop him without sacrificing you and the future we planned together."

She slowly shook her head. "Had you confronted him, you wouldn't have stopped him. He was hell-bent. A confrontation only would have spurred him on. You and Gray merely would have allowed yourself to be consumed in the fire he built. *Everyone* we loved would have been destroyed. I knew that fact the very night he came to me, and it was proven to me dozens of times in the years that followed. I *had* to protect you from him and from yourself."

"By ripping my heart to shreds?" he asked, moving toward her.

He had never allowed her to know how deeply he had been cut by her leaving. She'd seen glimpses, of course, in the time they'd been reunited, but he had tucked a great deal of it away. But now she knew it all, from the horrible hours on the terrace when he'd considered ending his life to the way he still bled for her loss.

She closed her eyes, and he could see an equal version of his pain reflected on her beautiful face.

"I know you love your family," she whispered. "Had you lost Felicity to the truth coming out, if everything you were fighting to rebuild in terms of reputation and finances was shattered around you, I know it would have hurt you more than my leaving did."

He caught his breath at the ignorance of that statement. He moved toward her, catching her in his arms and dragging her against him. Her eyes flew open and she stared up at him in surprise.

"When you walked away, it was the defining moment of my life, Elise. Perhaps you didn't believe that would be true, but I am telling you now that it is. Nothing in this world could have been worse than the moment you were gone. So please don't pretend that it was a better choice."

Her lip trembled. "I didn't know."

He nodded. "I realize that. But I also realize now that you didn't trust me."

"It wasn't my place to tell Felicity's secret," she offered, but her voice was weak.

"Perhaps not. But it was your place to tell me that you were being threatened. That you were being blackmailed. That you were in danger, for it was my place to protect you. But you didn't. And even when we reconnected, you *still* didn't trust me. Why?"

She struggled with that answer for a moment, seeking words to explain when he knew full well that there were none. There could never be any.

"How would it have helped once we were together again? You hated me. You had no faith in me and I understood why. If I'd told you earlier, it wouldn't have changed what I did to you. You might not have even believed me. It certainly would have seemed self-serving. Besides, I..." She turned her face. "I deserved your hatred, Lucien. I *deserved* it."

He let her go, shocked by that answer. He backed up a step. "Are you truly telling me that but for this renewed threat toward my family, you would have kept this secret forever?"

She nodded slowly.

He turned and walked to the window, staring out with unseeing eyes as he clenched and unclenched his hands at his sides. He was trying to process this, trying to understand just how far they'd come from two people in love to two people who had been thrown so far apart.

"So you still don't trust me," he muttered.

She caught her breath behind him and whispered, "Lucien—"

He cut her off by facing her and saying, "You know that the new Kirkford, he doesn't only threaten us with his desire to find your husband's information. It's evident from his physical attack on you that you are at a great risk, as well."

She swallowed and he saw the fear in her eyes as she thought of the man who had assaulted her less than twenty-four hours before. "Yes."

"Do you really think Winstead can protect you from

Kirkford's intentions?" he asked, all but spitting out the other man's name.

She shifted, and he could see the answer before she formulated it. "If—if he understood the situation," she whispered. "If he understood *how* to do it."

Stenfax waved a hand. "He's damned pup, Elise."

She bent her head and color flooded her cheeks. "He is young, yes."

"Christ, you tell him this story and he may not even keep you regardless of any arrangements you made or any...connection you created if you bedded him." Saying those words turned his stomach.

Her eyes went wide. "I did *not* bed him, Lucien," she said, her tone strangled. "If I had, I never would have come here. I would have stayed out on the street rather than asked you for help if I'd gone so far."

He almost sagged in relief at that statement. "Good," he whispered.

"Good that I would have stayed away, or good that I haven't bedded him?" she said, folding her arms, her eyes flashing.

He moved toward her. "The thought of any other man touching you has always driven me to the brink, Elise. Why do you think I reacted so strongly to your headstrong notion about becoming a mistress?"

"I still see it as my only true viable option, Lucien," she said, throwing up her hands. "By dragging me out into Society, Ambrose damaged me. And even if he hadn't, a courtship to a marriage could take months, even years. I don't have that kind of time and I have no settlement to free myself from Ambrose. Becoming a mistress is a way to remain safe. You must know it is the only reason I would consider that path."

He folded his arms. She was right, of course. If he dismissed everything else, all the threats against his family, all the lies and mistrust between them, the facts were the facts. Elise was in grave, immediate danger from the new Duke of Kirkford, even more than his sister or the rest of his family.

And there were few options for her. Which meant there was only one option for him. A decision that hit him like a punch to the gut and nearly dropped him to the ground as he made it in an instant.

"There is one other option," he said softly.

"Then share it with me, Lucien. I will hear anything at this point."

He set his stance a little wider and cleared his throat as he croaked out the words.

"You could marry me."

CHAPTER SIXTEEN

Four years before Elise had walked onto the terrace at Stenfax's country home to find it strewn with rose petals and glowing with what had to be a thousand candles. The man she loved had lit up as she moved toward him, then dropped to his knees. He had poured out words of love, promises of a future, and had asked her to be his countess. She had agreed with no hesitation in her heart, naught but joy in her entire being. It had been one of the happiest nights of her life. One she had relived a hundred times in the desperation of the past three years.

Now she faced the same man asking the same question, and it took the air from her lungs. Lucien stood in an almost military stance, his face impassive, his voice calm. There were no flowers or declarations, just a simple suggestion to save her from danger. Like he was offering to escort her to the market or fetch her a cloak so she didn't freeze.

But when she looked in his eyes, she saw the torment there that he didn't speak. She dipped her head.

And yet he wanted to marry her.

Perhaps *wanted* was too strong a word.

"Are you going to say something?" he asked.

She caught her breath. "M-marry?" she whispered, knowing it sounded like idiotic parroting but unable to form any other coherent words in her current shocked state.

"Yes," he said, not breaking his cool, even stare.

"You cannot mean that," she said.

He arched a brow. "No? You know me so well?"

She tensed. The truth of this man was so very clear and so very decent. "I know you well enough to know you wouldn't ask this if you didn't mean it," she admitted.

He nodded.

"But I want you tell me why you offer this, especially considering the last three years. Hell, the last three hours," she said.

He sighed, and his voice was soft as he said, "To protect you. If Kirkford is so driven, you'll be at risk as much as or more than Felicity is. And considering the sacrifice you made all those years ago to keep us safe, I cannot allow that."

Pain rushed through her, even though she'd already guessed his answer. Somehow she'd hoped he would look at her and see her as the same woman he'd once loved. That he would touch her and connect with her. That he'd allow himself to care even just a little.

"We could find another way," she whispered.

He stiffened. "You still wish to escape a union with me, Elise?"

"No!" she cried, stepping toward him. "I never did, Lucien."

His expression softened just a fraction. "Yes, I know. I'm sorry, that was uncalled for." He glided a hand through his hair, and suddenly she saw a thousand cracks in his emotionless mask. "I don't know what else to do, Elise. I could become your protector, certainly, but there wouldn't be as much safety in that role. You wouldn't live in my home, with my name wrapped around you. And there is also the fact that this morning, when we made love, we weren't *careful*. So that means not only you could be in danger, but my..."

He caught his breath and she did the same. "Your child," she finished, trying not to picture that very child in her mind.

He jerked out a trembling nod. "Yes," he whispered. "I would never allow any child of mine to be threatened, no matter how small the possibility that a baby now exists. As my wife, I could give you more layers of security."

143

Everything he said made perfect sense, and it had the added advantage that she would be his wife, the place where she'd always wanted to be. And yet there was little joy for her in the notion, because it wasn't born of love.

She reached for him and he allowed her to take his hand. She held it gently, reveling in the superior size, the rougher quality. These hands had brought her such pleasure. And she wanted them to bring her so much more. But she also wanted these hands to touch her in love, not just desire. She wanted these hands to hold their children, without a barrier between them born of the past.

"I asked you a question the last time we were at Vivien's," she said, gathering up her courage as best she could. "I asked you if we could start over. You told me you couldn't trust me. After today, has that changed?"

He pulled his hand from hers, but didn't step away. Instead, he cupped her cheek, smoothing his fingers along the skin, ultimately gentle. He locked eyes with her and whispered, "Elise, *you* didn't trust *me*. So as much as I'd love to start over, until we can trust *each other*, it's still impossible."

She shut her eyes, pain flowing through her veins, through her muscles, through her bones. "But you'll still marry me," she whispered.

"If you agree," he said. "And it won't have to be unhappy."

She almost laughed at that idea that she could be his wife, without his love or his trust, and be happy. But she didn't. This was her only way out now. He was right about that. And perhaps if they were together, she could one day prove herself worthy of his heart again.

It was better than an empty life alone, going from protector to protector and only wanting Lucien in the depths of her heart.

"I'll marry you," she whispered.

She opened her eyes to find him staring at her. He wasn't smiling, but his gaze was intense, focused, driven.

"Did you say yes?" he asked, his tone filled with disbelief.

She nodded. "Yes, Lucien."

He bent his head then and caught her in a kiss so soft and gentle that it melted away some of her disappointment. If they had nothing else, they would have this. This physical connection, this beating desire between them. She would fight the rest of her days to obtain the rest.

He was worth the fight.

He drew back at last and stepped away, the wall coming back between them.

"What will you do about Kirkford and the potential for this book?" she asked, hoping her disappointment wasn't too evident.

Lucien blew out a breath with a shake of his head. "I don't know. We'll work it out, though. We'll just find a way." He reached for her hand. "Now come, there is much to do and much to say now that this decision has been made."

She let him lead her from the room, down the hallway to where the others waited. Even though his hand was in hers, she still felt distant from it all.

Distant as they stepped into the room and the others faced them. Distant as Lucien said, "I have an announcement. Elise and I will wed as soon as I can get the special license."

There was a stunned silence in the room, not that Elise had expected anything else. These people had all hated her less than an hour before. They stared, and then it was Gray's wife Rosalinde who reacted first.

"How wonderful," she said, her voice tight. She moved across the room and kissed Stenfax's cheek, then turned to Elise. "With all the excitement, we have never actually been officially introduced. I'm Rosalinde. And I'm *very* happy to know you."

She leaned in and surprised Elise by folding her into a warm and welcoming embrace. Elise went limp in it for a moment, clinging to this woman who had not been part of the past she once shared with Stenfax and Gray and Felicity.

"You did a brave thing," Rosalinde whispered before she pulled away.

Her reaction opened the floodgates and Gray stepped up

145

next. He shook Stenfax's hand solemnly and then reached for Elise. The hatred she'd seen in him just a few days before was muted now. He was still standoffish, but that was Gray. He did not forgive easily.

"This is the right thing," he said, as close to an acceptance as he would likely make for now. "Thank you for what you did for my sister."

When he stepped away, Felicity approached next. She was shaking, her eyes still wide and filled with terror at the dark future she would possibly encounter.

"I should have done more," Elise said.

Felicity shook her head. "You did all you could. More than you should have. And I am glad to be able to rebuild our friendship. There were so many times over the years that *you* were the one I wanted to talk to."

That admission brought tears rushing to Elise's eyes and she caught Felicity in a brief hug.

Stenfax cleared his throat. "I'd like to talk to Gray. Why don't you ladies take a moment?"

Elise turned on him, catching his arm. "Oh, please don't shut me out of whatever you're planning, Lucien. I could help and—"

"I won't," he said softly. He met her stare and she swallowed hard as she thought of what he'd said earlier. That until they could rebuild the faith between them, there was no starting over.

And this was the first test.

She released him and he moved toward the door with Gray as she said, "I trust you."

She saw his shoulders stiffen, pushing back, but he didn't stop. The two just left the room together. Elise sighed as they did. She hadn't been able to have faith in anyone, even herself, for so long.

It would take practice to do so again. And patience to rebuild what she'd lost with the man she loved.

Stenfax shut his office door softly, and before he could even face his brother, Gray barked out, "Bloody hell, Lucien."

Stenfax nodded, knowing Gray referred to every terrible thing that had happened in the past short while. Their entire lives had been turned upside down with just a few words.

"Yes, bloody hell sums it up just about perfectly," Stenfax said as he moved to the sideboard and splashed scotch into two glasses. As he held out a glass to his brother, he said, "And now what do we do about this? *All* of this?"

Gray ignored the offering of the liquor as he paced the room, his demeanor like a caged animal. Stenfax knew how he felt. "Kirkford must be dealt with."

Stenfax swigged the first scotch and set it down before he gripped his fist. "I want to ride over there and tear him limb from limb for what he did to Elise."

Gray stepped toward him, laying a calming hand on his arm. "I understand the drive, brother, I assure you. When Rosalinde's grandfather attacked her last year, I would have killed him without a second thought. But in this case, turning on the man will do us no good. He'll only be more driven to find this book of secrets and use it against us."

Stenfax tapped his foot restlessly. "I know you're right, but he...he tried to rape her, Gray."

"But he didn't succeed," Gray said. "And his threats have led us to the truth at last."

Stenfax pulled from his brother's touch. He knew Gray was right, of course. But the idea of letting it be, at least for now, was repugnant.

"So what *do* we do?"

"Celia married a former agent of the crown," Gray suggested.

Stenfax nodded. Celia was Rosalinde's sister and his own former fiancée. Their thwarted nuptials had led Gray and

Rosalinde to each other, and he considered Celia a friend. Her new marriage to a former spy, one who had until recently been masquerading as a duke, was not known to anyone but their immediate family.

"John Dane *could* help. At least we know he could be trusted to guide us," Stenfax admitted. "How long would it take for him to get here?"

Gray shrugged. "A week, perhaps. He won't like coming to London, though. The case where he met Celia is still fresh and he would likely fear it could endanger her if he was seen here."

"When I marry Elise, the ripples through Society will be massive. It might be best to do it swiftly and in the country, at Caraway Court. We can regroup there and make our longer term plans."

"Dane would prefer it, I'm sure. And Celia will be happy to see Rosalinde and offer her support to Elise and to you," Gray said. "I'll send Dane word and ask them to meet us there in a fortnight."

"A fortnight?" Stenfax burst out. "That's a bloody long time to let Ambrose go unchecked."

Gray held up his hands. "I understand your issue, but what can we do? As far as we know, he doesn't have the book right now. He's still searching and until he has it, anything he says or does will only make him look like a fool."

"So you bank on the even-headedness of man who tried to rape my fiancée." Stenfax gripped and ungripped his fist at his side.

"I think we have to be even keeled if he will not. That means taking our time and doing what we need to do with the proper thought," Gray said, softer, to counteract Stenfax's loudness. "Your special license will take some doing, we must move to the countryside and Dane must have time to do some research so he can come to us with his ideas on the subject."

Stenfax bent his head. Of course his brother was right. If he railed and roared and caused chaos it would not help anyone. "In the meantime, Elise can help us assemble a list of names of people her late husband abused. It might help us trace the book."

"Yes, the more we know, the better it will be for us." Gray stopped pacing and looked at him. "And so you'll really marry her?"

Stenfax stiffened. Gray had had so little reaction to the announcement in the parlor a few moments before, and now his voice was calm and collected. Lucien had no idea if his brother was shocked or horrified or angry or supportive. He didn't like being in the dark.

"To protect her, I feel it is the only way," Stenfax said, his own voice just as noncommittal.

Gray gave him a half-smile. "And it has nothing to do with the fact that you love her. That you never stopped loving her."

Stenfax sucked in a huge breath. Now that it had been said out loud, the truth of it weaseled past the walls he'd built so long ago to protect himself. He leaned with both hands on his desk as his head swam and his body swayed.

"Yes," he admitted at last. "There is also that."

"I did not think getting you to admit it would be so simple."

Stenfax almost laughed, even though this didn't feel funny in the slightest. "I wouldn't say it is simple, just too powerful to deny."

Gray tilted his head. "Yes, it always is when it's so real and so strong. But you're not happy about the marriage, it seems."

Stenfax stared at his cluttered desktop with unseeing eyes. "Elise and I have spent years not trusting each other. How could we possibly build a happy life on that bad beginning?"

Gray's laugh was swift and unexpected. "I suppose I am the perfect person to ask, aren't I? After all, Rosalinde and I started out without any trust between us. I thought her sister a title hunter, she thought me cruel and manipulative. Despite all that, we worked it out."

"But it's not the same," Stenfax said, even though that reminder of Gray and Rosalinde's start was somewhat comforting and hopeful.

"No?" Gray asked. "I suppose not. After all, you've been in

love with Elise for what...over a decade?"

"No—"

"And you planned to marry her once before, under very different circumstances."

Lucien huffed out a breath of frustration. "But—"

Gray tilted his head, unrelenting. "And she sacrificed herself to a marriage that sounds only slightly less awful than our own sister's to save Felicity. To save *you*."

"I know!" Stenfax burst out when Gray let him have a word. "But if I'd known—"

Gray held up a hand. "But we don't get to walk that path, Lucien. The path where you knew the truth from the beginning is gone. *This* is the path now. You can live in what might have been or could have been or should have been and I don't think anyone would blame you. But if you have any hope to be happy, not just with Elise, but with yourself, you must live in what is now, *today*."

"I don't know if I can," Stenfax whispered, though Gray's words were like a beacon through a fog.

Gray moved forward and clapped a hand on Lucien's shoulder. "Not many people get a second chance like this. Think about it, will you?"

Stenfax sighed as his brother changed the subject, back to how they would protect Felicity. Gray's words meant a great deal to him.

And he knew he would think about them, only about them, for a good while to come.

CHAPTER SEVENTEEN

Elise had learned a great deal in the short moments she'd had alone with Rosalinde and Felicity. Mostly, she realized just how kind and good a person Rosalinde was. While some women would have turned up their nose at her, especially after all the shocking things that had come out about her past, Rosalinde was gentle and welcoming. She had even tried to ease the awkward reconnection between Felicity and Elise.

But at last she rose. "You know, I'd like to speak to Xavier about something. Why don't the two of you keep talking? I'll be back shortly."

She waved at then to keep their seats as she left and closed the door behind her. Elise smiled at Felicity. "She's lovely."

Felicity nodded instantly. "She truly is. Gray adores her almost to distraction."

Elise's eyes went wide as she thought of the stern, quiet Gray she'd known as a girl. "I wouldn't have thought he'd ever allow himself that kind of connection."

"No, we all worried he would block himself off from it, but Rosalinde is everything to him." Felicity smiled broadly. "We're lucky to have her in our family. And her sister, Celia, is just as delightful."

Elise froze. "Celia, the one Stenfax was to marry," she said slowly.

Felicity leaned in and caught Elise's hands. "He *never* cared for her. Nor she for him. It was entirely a match of convenience and I think both were relieved when the engagement ultimately ended."

Elise shook her head in utter disbelief. "I don't know how she couldn't have loved Lucien if she spent any length of time with him."

Felicity expression softened at that observation. "Perhaps she simply sensed that he wasn't truly free. After all, he was still connected to you."

"By his hate," Elise said.

"No," Felicity said, squeezing her fingers gently before she released her. "Not his hate, even if he would have labeled it as that for a long time. Either way, Celia recently married and seems very happy where she is. It all worked out for the best, for now you will marry my brother."

Elise caught her breath at that matter-of-fact statement. It sounded so very shocking to her ears, even though it had been decided almost an hour before. She was not in any way accustomed to it.

"Are you *truly* happy about that fact?" Elise asked at last, shooting her friend a side glance.

Felicity bent her head. "If you had asked me that question this morning, I admit I would have said no. I would have been horrified by the very notion that Lucien would tie himself to you again and in such a permanent way. But now that the truth has come out, I feel differently. In fact, I feel joyful. You sacrificed your future with him once to save me. Now this fixes that bitter action. It resets the world, in a way."

Elise pressed her lips together hard before she said, "I'm not sure about that. It certainly doesn't fix or change what I did to Lucien."

"You don't think he forgives you, even after you told him why you did what you did?"

Elise considered the question, rolling it around in her mind to see if it fit her sense of discomfort. Her mind was such a jumble, it was hard to determine the truth in it all.

"It isn't that he hasn't forgiven me," she said at last. "I think he is beginning to do that. More that he is resigned to this marriage as a way to somehow repay me for my sacrifice all those years ago."

Felicity's expression grew concerned. "You know Lucien."

"I did once, yes."

"He hasn't changed that much," her friend reassured her. "He's...*guarded* when he isn't certain. Everything just came out today, Elise. His entire world, his entire system of belief, has been turned on its head. You must let him settle into it, think on it, find a way to accept what happened all those years ago. His heart will soften in time."

Elise got up and paced away, hands shaking at her sides. "Only I don't know if it can. He tells me over and over that our lack of trust is what keeps us apart and I cannot argue that point. Trust cannot just be magically obtained."

Felicity jumped up. "I can help. After all, it's just about *earning* his trust, isn't it? I'll help you find a way to do that."

Elise sighed. "That isn't the issue at present. Lucien believes I don't trust *him*. And I have no idea how to prove that I do."

Felicity looked just as stumped as she was, but before they could speak more on the subject, the parlor door opened and Rosalinde and Gray entered the chamber, followed by Lucien, himself. His gaze swept over the room and when he found her, his shoulders stiffened and the line of his lips thinned.

Both those things made her stomach drop. He had secured her future with his proposal, but it didn't feel secure right now. Not when he clearly hesitated, forced into a corner by her circumstances.

"My dear, I've been thinking, and while you obviously had little choice given what happened last night, you cannot stay with Stenfax during your engagement," Rosalinde said. "Why don't you come and stay with Gray and me?"

Elise looked at Stenfax once again. Of course, what Rosalinde said was proper, but she wanted to see if it disappointed him as much as it disappointed her.

But his expression was unreadable.

"Oh, no, she should come stay with Mother and me!" Felicity said, grabbing for Elise's arm.

Gray smiled at his sister. "Normally I would agree that you two should have time to reconnect as friends. But given the threat that still exists toward Elise, until we leave London for Caraway Court, it would be best if she were under my roof. I can make sure she's protected."

Felicity's own smile fell and the gravity of the situation felt very clear in that moment. "Of course," she said, her voice strained.

Elise squeezed her arm gently before she stepped toward Lucien. "Caraway Court?" she asked.

He nodded. "Gray and I thought it best to regroup there. Plan our next moves. Do you oppose the idea?"

Elise shrugged, partly because she didn't think any objection she had would matter, but also because she had such fond memories of Caraway Court. It was where she'd first fallen in love with the man who would now reluctantly become her husband.

Perhaps there she would find a way to remind him that he'd once loved her too.

"I don't mind leaving London," she said. "I'm sure the scandal when our engagement is announced will be massive. I don't want to be in the center of that storm."

"Then it sounds like Elise *trusts* you with your decision, Lucien," Felicity said, sending her brother a meaningful look.

Elise held back a sigh. Of course Felicity would try to solve this problem, even in the clumsiest way. Stenfax's expression didn't change even though he looked at Elise a little closer.

She forced a smile. "I suppose I should have my maid prepare us for another move. Not that there is much for Ruth to prepare. I left with so few things."

"Do you think the servants at the dower house would help get the rest of your clothing out?" Stenfax asked.

She nodded. "There are many there who are sympathetic to my plight. As long as Ambrose hasn't burned my belongings already, it's possible."

"I'll go get them," Stenfax said.

Gray stepped forward. "You damned well won't. Remember what we discussed regarding confronting the man? We'll send a few servants. You'll stay right where you are so you don't end up killing a duke and putting us in an even more precarious position." Felicity flinched and Gray turned toward her. "I'm sorry, Felicity. I wasn't thinking."

She shrugged. "You're right, though. My actions have placed us all in danger and we must act carefully."

Lucien tapped his foot, frustration clear on his face. He was a man of action and his hands were tied. Yet another thing Elise knew was her fault.

"Very well," he ground out. "I'll send servants. I hate having no options here."

She turned her face. No options in anything, it seemed, even a wedding. "Yes, well, I'll go prepare Ruth. I won't be long."

She turned to leave the room and was surprised when Lucien followed her without an explanation or a request to the others for leave. In the hall, she turned toward him.

"Lucien—" she began softly.

His face remained impassive. "What will you do in regards to Winstead?"

She blinked. Here she had hoped he followed her in order to comfort her or to connect with her. Instead he asked about the man who would have been her lover.

She swallowed hard. "I hadn't thought about it. I suppose he must be told that my plans have changed. Writing him seems cruel."

Stenfax lifted his chin. "It is what you did to me."

She caught her breath. "Because Kirkford orchestrated my actions in order to cause the most pain he could."

He seemed to consider that for a long moment, then he nodded. "We don't want to inspire the man to become another enemy. Right now there are plenty of complications without that. But I don't want you to go to him. You were already physically threatened and I can't have you face his anger."

"You think he'll be angry?" she asked.

He shrugged. "How could he not be, losing you?" She gasped at the assessment, but he didn't allow her to respond. "Let me go speak to him. Then if you wish to write a letter afterward, I won't object."

She tensed. Her...well, she supposed she could call Stenfax her fiancé now...her fiancé and the man who had offered as her protector. She couldn't imagine *that* meeting would go well. Especially since Stenfax felt so unable to do anything about Ambrose. Winstead could very well suffer the consequences he didn't deserve.

"Don't take your anger out on him," she whispered. "Please promise me that."

He arched a brow. "Worried about him, are we?"

"No," she said, hating his sharp tone. "Worried about you. Only you, Lucien."

She leaned up and briefly brushed her lips to his cheek, then turned toward stairs and away from Lucien. Away from the feelings he no longer felt. Away from the future that she'd once so longed for, but now felt locked in painful stone.

Lucien sat in a quiet parlor, awaiting the arrival of a man who did not expect him. To give him news that could set him off in God knew what ways. He probably shouldn't have been the one giving this news, given the fact that he would now wed Elise.

But he felt impotent in this situation. He had bid farewell to her an hour before, watching her ride off in Gray's carriage with her head bent. He had not allowed himself to touch her, to really connect with her, as she left his house as his fiancée.

It seemed there was more of a wall between them than there had ever been, and he shifted in discomfort at that acknowledgment to himself. This wasn't what he wanted, but he had no idea how to fix it.

The door to the parlor opened and he rose slowly to watch Theodore Winstead enter the room. The younger man looked calm in the face of his uninvited presence and shut the door quietly behind him.

"My lord," he said, his tone only a touch wary.

"Winstead," he replied, forcing some level of common politeness as he extended a hand. "Thank you for seeing me." Winstead nodded as he shook Stenfax's hand. Then they sat. "I assume you know why I'm here."

Winstead tilted his head. "I can only hazard a guess that this is about the Duchess of Kirkford."

"Yes," Stenfax said softly, examining the man closely for his reaction. How much did he want Elise? And how far had things truly gone between them? "It is about Elise."

Winstead stood with a sigh and crossed to the sideboard where he poured two whiskeys. "I think we could both use these to buoy us through what seems is going to be a very uncomfortable discussion."

"I know you offered to be her protector," Stenfax said flatly.

Winstead froze in the midst of pouring and said, "I see."

"It isn't going to happen," Stenfax said, bracing for whatever reaction Winstead might have to that statement.

There was none for a moment, but then Winstead turned. His expression was clear of any emotion, though he held Stenfax's gaze evenly. He handed over the drink and Stenfax took it, though he didn't drink. He wanted a very clear head in this moment and it was already clouded enough by jealousy.

"No?" Winstead said as he retook his seat calmly.

Stenfax shook his head slowly. "No. Elise is going to marry *me*."

Winstead was silent for what felt like an eternity, and then said, "Is that what she told you, or is it merely your hope that she will agree?"

Stenfax stared. There was no fear in this young man, despite

Stenfax's superior title and what he knew was his bad attitude. He found himself rather liking Winstead, despite himself.

"I asked her this morning," he said softly. "And she agreed."

For the first time, Winstead frowned, and he set his drink on the table beside him. "She never mentioned that was a possibility."

Stenfax shrugged. "Likely because she didn't realize it was. Circumstances have changed and this is the best way forward for her. For us."

Winstead examined him closely and then said, "Well, I can see why she would inspire such an action. She's a remarkable woman."

Stenfax tensed, gripping the chair arms with both hands as he fought every violent tendency that rushed through his body. "Yes," he ground out.

Winstead arched a brow. "I never touched her beyond a kiss, Stenfax. And even that she hardly returned. I recognized her hesitance. I hoped once day she would overcome her reticence, but it seems it wasn't meant to be."

Stenfax blinked as those words sank in. Elise had said the same to him, that she had never bedded this man. He realized, in a horrible flash of truth, that some part of him had doubted her words. Some tiny inch still doubted *her*, even though he knew her motivations in leaving him all those years ago.

It seemed old habits died hard.

"She's in danger, isn't she?" Winstead asked, breaking into Stenfax's thoughts.

He set his jaw, almost as troubled by the fact that Elise might have confided in this man as he was that she could have been with him. "Did she tell you that?"

"No. Not exactly. She implied her situation was precarious, but nothing more. The new Duke of Kirkford's behavior toward her is obvious. When he dragged her to Lord and Lady Swinton's party in a gown more suited for Vivien's parlor than a proper one, it was clear he wished to destroy her. And then there is the fear that always seems to be in Elise's eyes." Winstead's eyes narrowed. "I'm not a fool. I know she's being threatened."

Stenfax clenched the chair arms again. "Yes," he admitted softly. "She is. The new duke is just as bad as the old one. She has not been safe in years, it seems."

"He's been heard around the clubs, you know, claiming there is some secret about her. Actually, he claims to be looking for access to the secrets of many a person. Especially when he's drunk."

Stenfax couldn't mask his surprise that this man who'd wanted to be her lover would be so direct with the man who'd stolen her from him. "Did he say what he knew about Elise?"

"No. And right now I don't think anyone believes him. He's seen as a pathetic lout, truth be told."

Stenfax let out a low sigh of relief. "I hope it stays that way," he murmured. "I also hope you won't turn whatever anger you may feel at losing her against her."

Winstead tilted his head. "I'll admit losing her stings a bit. But I'll survive it. And I don't think Elise deserves the censure or fear I think she's endured. Not from Kirkford...not from *anyone*."

Stenfax flinched, for the accusation was obvious in the young man's tone. And that it was deserved, was the worst part. He had no defense over the truth.

"Well, I thank you for that promise. And for your kindness toward my future wife when she so obviously needed it. Good day, Winstead."

He bowed stiffly and Winstead got up to follow him in to the foyer. They shook hands once more there, and Winstead said, "I truly hope you can find a way to make Elise happy. And yourself. It seems, after so long being separated that you both deserve that. Good day."

Stenfax's horse was brought around then and Winstead strode off, leaving Stenfax to digest what he'd said.

Elise didn't deserve what had happened. Elise didn't

deserve to be threatened. Elise didn't deserve to be abused. No, she did not. So he turned his horse toward not his own house, but another one.

And knew he'd break a promise he'd made not only to Elise, but to his brother.

CHAPTER EIGHTEEN

The cart he'd sent with two of his largest footmen was pulling onto the drive at Elise's dower house when he arrived. He rode his horse to the edge of the entryway and was readying himself to get down when he heard a rustle in the bushes beside him and his name whispered on the wind.

"Stenfax."

He turned to find Gray moving onto the street. His brother folded his arms and arched a brow at him.

"Bloody hell," Stenfax muttered as he placed his feet on the ground. "Did you follow me?"

"No," Gray said. "Not followed. Just anticipated you'd do something so foolhardy. What are you thinking coming here, Lucien, after what we discussed earlier in the day at your home?"

Stenfax gripped his hands at his sides as rage boiled up in him. Rage he had controlled for a long time but now broke free.

"I will not turn tail and run away from a man who dared place his hands on the woman I love. Who dares to threaten my sister. I stood by idly for years, knowing his cousin had stolen all I held dear. Now I'm expected to send servants to collect Elise's things, just to make sure I won't offend that bastard of a new duke if he's here? This is too damned much."

Gray let out a sigh. "Is there any turning you from this path?"

"No," Lucien said softly.

Gray nodded. "Well, I assumed there would not be. Come

then, let's go."

Lucien leaned back. "You're going with me?"

Gray chuckled. "Someone has to protect Kirkford."

They exchanged a nod, then entered the drive as Stenfax's footmen began their way up the steps. Both the servants looked surprised to see their master and gave bows.

"My lord?" the head footman said. "I-I didn't realize—"

Stenfax held up a hand to stay him. "I know, thank you. Why don't you and Cummings take the cart around back? I'll have you let in there to do the moving."

The men nodded and went back to their cart to move it. Stenfax drew a long breath, put his coldest expression on and knocked. A butler answered the door in a moment.

"May I help you?" he asked, his tone and demeanor harried.

"I'm here to retrieve the Duchess of Kirkford's things," he said, pushing past the man. "Have my servants let in and show them to her chamber."

The servant gave a faint smile but then pushed it aside. "I see, sir." He leaned in. "I must offer up some resistance, you know."

Stenfax stiffened. "Does that mean the duke is in residence?" he whispered.

"In the west parlor, drinking and tearing down anything Her Grace decorated with. Also stoking the fire to burn her clothes."

Stenfax clenched his fists, and Gray set a hand on his arm gently. "Make your arguments," Gray suggested. "Loudly, and we will push past and go confront the duke. While we do so, allow the men in. They're large. They overpowered you."

The butler nodded, then stepped back and shouted, "What are you doing here? I don't care who you are, you can't just barge in here demanding to take my master's things!"

Stenfax smiled and folded a coin into his fingers. "Thank you."

"You're certainly welcome, my lord," the man said as he motioned for them to go to the parlor. He trailed behind as they did so and as Stenfax pushed the door open, he said, "I'm sorry,

Your Grace, they couldn't be stopped."

As they stepped into the room, all three of them stopped and the butler jerked a hand to his mouth with a gasp. The new Duke of Kirkford was not thrashing about the room as had been described, exacting revenge on Elise's belongings.

Instead he was lying on the floor before the fireplace, a knife sticking out of his chest.

Gray rushed forward, dropping to his knees before the man. "He's still alive," he cried out. "Call for the guard and a doctor!"

The butler ran to do so, leaving Stenfax and Gray to the duke. Stenfax moved forward, staring at the face of his enemy. The new duke had as cruel a face as the last one, and he couldn't feel sorry that he'd been attacked.

Gray looked up at him. "It's bad," he murmured.

Kirkford moaned. "I can't breathe," he panted.

"The blood is filling his lungs," Stenfax said as he observed the position of the knife. "I don't think there's much that can be done."

Kirkford's eyes went wide with fear. Slowly Stenfax sank to his haunches and looked him in the eye. "You tried to hurt Elise, so I feel no pity for you. But I will try to bring you justice, not that you deserve it. Who did this to you?"

Kirkford was gasping for air now, and there was a wheezing, sucking sound to it. "My—my cousin, Roger," he managed weakly. "We were born on the same day, he challenged me as heir to the dukedom. He never got over that I won."

Gray and Stenfax exchanged a look. "You told Elise there was a book," Gray said, placing a hand on Stenfax's chest to keep him from talking. He understood why, Gray was more likely to massage the information out of Kirkford than he was. "Where is it?"

Kirkford coughed and blood trickled from his mouth and nose. But he still smiled, a disgusting, red-toothed grin. "You're afraid of the book? You should be. I know it has secrets. I…found   it.
Would…have…destroyed…when…I…understood." His words

came slower now, more labored as he drowned in his blood. "Roger...took...it..."

He sucked in one last breath and then it all hissed out. He stopped moving, and he was gone.

"Goddamn it!" Stenfax roared, getting to his feet and scrubbing a hand through his hair. "So now the book isn't hidden, it's in the wild."

Gray slid a hand over the duke's eyes, closing them gently before he got to his feet. "What did he mean by 'when I understood'?"

"I don't know," Stenfax said. "Perhaps he didn't have time to read it before Roger came and killed him, taking it with him?"

"That doesn't make sense," Gray said. Then he pointed toward the body. "Look, what's that in his hand?"

Stenfax crouched down again and saw what his brother indicated. A piece of torn paper sticking out of Kirkford's clenched fist. He pried his fingers open gently and pulled it loose. They held it up together, looking at it. It was an odd jumble of letters, not spelling out anything Stenfax understood."

The brothers exchanged a look. "It's code," Stenfax said. "The book is in code, *that's* what Kirkford meant."

"And since he didn't understand, I think we can safely assume that Roger would need to break it, as well, before he could use it against anyone, including Felicity."

A small fraction of relief pierced the horrified feeling in Stenfax's chest. "So we may have some time," he murmured.

"A little, anyway," Gray said. "We should take this to the Earl of Stalwood. He worked with Dane for years. He can help us with the code."

He shoved the paper in his pocket just as members of the guard burst into the room and chaos descended. Stenfax stepped away as they approached and began to question them. His score with the new Duke of Kirkford had been settled, but he felt no joy in it. Elise might be safer, but now he would have to tell her, and Felicity, that this mysterious book was out there.

And he didn't look forward to that.

Elise watched Rosalinde pace the parlor, looking at the clock over and over again. "I have no idea why Gray is so late."

"He is never late?"

Rosalinde shook her head. "Not without sending me word. And he looked very…well, he was acting suspiciously when he departed, so I wonder what trouble he's gotten into."

"Come sit," Elise said, patting the settee beside her. When Rosalinde did so, she turned in her place a little to face her. "I knew Gray as a boy, you know."

Rosalinde's worried expression softened a little. "Yes, I know. He has told me many a tale of you and Felicity following him and Stenfax and Asher around."

"I'm sure until recently I was a reluctant part of those stories, considering his feelings for me," Elise said.

Rosalinde squeezed her hand. "Gray is the most loyal brother I've ever met. He fought hard against Stenfax's marriage to my sister just because he felt you had hurt Stenfax in the past. It nearly tore us apart."

Elise smiled at her. "But you survived. And I will tell you that thinking of the boy I knew all those years ago, I never would have thought he would be capable of the love I see him display with you, Rosalinde. You have truly captured his heart and made him a different person."

"I hope that is not true, for I adore the person he is in every way. Flaws and all, just as he does me." Rosalinde tilted her head. "Perfection is not required, nor is molding ourselves to be something new or never making a mistake. But owning up to our mistakes is paramount. Which is what you did today."

Elise sighed. "And I got an engagement to a man who doesn't know what to do with me out of it."

"You love him," Rosalinde said softly.

Elise looked at her. Unlike Felicity or Gray or Stenfax, she had no history with this woman. Nothing preconceived or bitter from the years that had separated them. And there was something in Rosalinde's kind and beautiful face that inspired honesty.

"I never stopped loving him," Elise admitted, her breath catching. "Never once in all this time. *That* was my prison, not anything that bastard Kirkford ever did or created."

"You *will* overcome this," Rosalinde whispered.

The door to the parlor opened and Gray entered, followed by Stenfax. Both women jumped to their feet, though for Rosalinde it was in relief. Elise was just surprised. Stenfax hadn't seemed to want to see her again today, and yet he was here, staring at her evenly.

"Where in the world were you?" Rosalinde asked as she kissed Gray openly and rather shamelessly.

He let her for a moment, then pulled back with a grim look for Stenfax. "I'll explain, but come with me. Stenfax must tell Elise something."

Elise stiffened as she stared at him. Tell her something? That couldn't mean anything good. Not when he looked slightly sick.

Rosalinde took Gray's arm, giving Elise one last concerned look before they left the parlor. As they shut the door, Elise stepped toward Stenfax.

"Are you ending our engagement?" she whispered.

His lips parted in surprise. "No, Elise. Of course not."

Relief flowed through her and she somehow managed to stay on her feet as her knees wobbled. Stenfax stepped closer, taking her elbow to steady her. That touch spread warmth through her entire body, and she looked up at him slowly.

He pressed his lips together. "Sit. This is...well, I don't know how you will take the news I've come to share."

She retook her place on the settee and he put himself next to her. Close enough that his leg brushed hers and set off a torrent of reaction through her body. He merely stared at her, though, as if he didn't know what to say.

"Did your meeting with Winstead go poorly?" she asked, hoping she could encourage him to explain.

He rubbed a hand over his face. "No, that actually went fine. You have nothing to fear from him, so it isn't that."

She rested a hand on his leg and squeezed. She felt his thigh muscle tighten against her hand and his pupils dilated slightly.

"What is it?" she whispered. "*Trust* me."

He caught his breath at the use of that word again. That word that hung between them. He nodded. "Yes, I must in this case. You deserve it. I know I agreed not to go to your dower house, Elise. But...I did."

She caught her breath. "Oh, Lucien. Was Ambrose there? Did you have a confrontation, did—"

"He's dead, Elise."

She stared at him a moment as his words sank in. Then she scooted back, as if she could separate herself from this horror. "No," she moaned, the sound low and pained and not expressing half the agony she felt. "Oh, please tell me you didn't, Lucien."

He caught her hands and held tight. "I didn't," he vowed. "I may have wanted to, but I wouldn't have for I knew it would only complicate this terrible situation. No, when Gray and I arrived, he was already...dying. He'd been stabbed. By his cousin."

Her lips parted. "Roger?"

"It seems their fight over the inheritance of the title was not yet finished."

She covered her mouth with both hands. "Oh God," she murmured through them. "When Toby died, their battle was terrible, yes, and they nearly came to blows several times during the legal proceedings that determined who was born first. But I never would have thought..."

"Apparently neither would Ambrose," Stenfax said softly.

"Then are we...safe?" she asked, a tiny flare of hope in her chest. She was embarrassed by it, that a man's death would inspire relief. Even a man she despised.

"Not exactly," he said. "Ambrose had found Kirkford's

book."

She stared. "He found it?"

Stenfax's face grew even more grim. "And Roger took it."

She leapt to her feet. "No! No, that cannot be. So the secrets are out? We are lost?"

"No." He stood and moved toward her, catching her and pulling her into his embrace. He smoothed her hair, tried to stay her trembling. But she couldn't stop, no matter how much his warmth pierced her and surrounded her.

"How could we not be?" she asked when she could find her words. "Roger is as cruel as his cousins ever were. In fact, he is a cold and calculated cruelty, not as wild as Toby and Ambrose were. Much more dangerous."

He winced at that assessment, but drew her back and looked down at her. "There was a page left behind in the struggle and it turns out Toby's book was encoded. Right now we don't believe Roger has a way to break the code. So that gives us some time."

She wrinkled her brow. "Coded?"

He nodded. "Yes. It seems your late husband wanted to protect the secrets he collected."

She bent her head. "So what do we do now?"

He smoothed a hand across her cheek. "The same thing we planned in the first place. You and I will marry, and we will look for the book. Roger is under suspicion for the murder of a duke. He'll be on the run. But we'll find him, and we'll find the book and destroy it. Nothing has changed."

She let out a shuddering sigh. "It doesn't feel like it. This whole day has been shifting sands beneath our feet. One enemy becomes another, truth becomes lies. Will we ever feel safe again?"

Suddenly his mouth was on hers. At first the kiss was gentle, but as she wound her arms around his neck, it grew more heated, more passionate. She sank into it, sank into him, and sighed as his tongue slid across hers. She felt the evidence of his desire for her, pressing firmly to her stomach, and wanted nothing more than to give in to it, give in to him.

After all, there was little she knew when it came to this man, but that they could connect so passionately, so sweetly, was one fact that had never changed.

He pulled away, and it was like he'd read her mind when he whispered, "There is nothing I'd like more than to lay you down on the settee and forget the madness of today. But it is getting late and we have somewhere to be."

She tilted her head. "Where?"

"My mother's. We'll go in the guise of telling her of our engagement. But while we're there, Gray and I will need to tell Felicity about the death of the Duke of Kirkford."

Elise shuddered. "She will be devastated."

"That's why I'm glad you'll be there to help," he said, holding her gaze steadily. "Now go up and change. Gray managed to convince the guard that we should take your clothing as we planned."

She blinked. He was offering her a little trust by asking her for her help with Felicity. She saw that. And though it was just a beginning, she would take it. Cling to it with both hands.

And pray she could one day manage to parlay it into a happy future.

CHAPTER NINETEEN

Lucien looked at Elise as she shifted in her seat, staring at the door where Felicity and his mother would soon join them and Gray and Rosalinde. The other couple was standing by the fire, their heads close together in private conversation.

Stenfax reached out and took Elise's hand, squeezing gently. "It's fine," he whispered.

Her already pale face drained further of color. "How can it be fine? Your mother must hate me as much as you and your siblings did."

Lucien frowned at her observation. She had lived in the shadow of his family's disdain for so long, now that she had been drawn out into the light it was like she didn't know what to do. That was his fault, he supposed. After all, she felt the walls between them.

He wanted so much to bring them down, but it wasn't so simple as that.

"Mama is an uncomplicated person," he said softly. "Will she be...*confused* by this change of events? I suppose she will. After all, I didn't hide my grief over losing you well, but she isn't the kind to turn away anyone. I assure you. Especially if Gray and Felicity show their support for the match."

The mention of his sister made Elise's face fall further. "Oh, how will Felicity take this news?" she whispered.

He tensed at the thought, but was happy to share his worries with someone who understood. "I'll have to draw her aside to tell her, and I admit I don't look forward to that moment."

"I'll help you as best I can," Elise said softly as she threaded her fingers through his. He looked down at her, soaking in the succor of her support, feeling the glow of his love for her in return.

Felicity entered the room and he drew away from Elise, rising to his feet as he faced his sister and his mother. Lady Stenfax smiled, but the expression slowly fell as she realized Elise was standing in her parlor.

"I—" she began. "Good Lord, Your Grace, I had no idea you would be joining the family for supper tonight."

"Lady Stenfax," Elise said, holding out a shaking hand toward his mother. "I hope my being here doesn't put you out overly much."

His mother blinked, and for a brief moment Stenfax though she might, indeed, refuse Elise. But then she put out her hand and caught Elise's gently. "Of course not, my dear. We will add another plate for supper. It has been..." She shot Stenfax a side glance. "...a very long time since we last saw you."

Stenfax cleared his throat as he sidled up to Elise and gently slipped an arm around her waist. He felt her lean into him a fraction and stroked his fingers against her side in some form of comfort. "Mama, I have news for you."

Lady Stenfax's eyes widened even further as she stared at the two of them. "I see that you do. What is going on?"

"Elise and I will wed," he said softly. "In Caraway Court, in two weeks' time."

It seemed the room held its collective breath as they awaited Lady Stenfax's reaction, but none more than Elise. He supposed he understood why. After all, she'd always liked his family, and since her own parents had both died during her marriage to Kirkford, she was quite alone in the world. He could imagine she would welcome the gentle presence of his mother.

"That's wonderful," Lady Stenfax said at last, and moved toward the couple to first kiss her son's cheek and then catch Elise's hands. "My dear, we have very much missed you in the company of our family. I only wish your parents were here to see this day. I know they wished for it."

Elise blinked in surprise. "You stayed in touch with my parents...*after*?"

Lady Stenfax wrinkled her brow. "Of course I did. I hope you got my note when they passed."

Elise swallowed hard. "I did, my lady. I am sorry I didn't write back—my grief was too much, I fear." She glanced at Stenfax with a soft smile. "But I did appreciate your kind words."

She was so lovely in that moment that it took everything in Stenfax not to grab her, sweep her over his shoulder and take her back to his home to lay claim to her right then and there. But he had one final unpleasant duty that night and it had to do with Felicity.

Lady Stenfax looked around the room with a shake of her head. "I can see that I am the last one to hear this news, am I? How did you all keep it a secret?"

Gray laughed. "Don't worry, Mama, it only just happened. You weren't kept in the dark long."

Elise cleared her throat. "I hate to bring up the obvious, but soon this news will spread far and wide. We cannot ignore the scandal it will create. So I would like to take a moment to apologize to you all for the trouble I may bring to your family."

Lady Stenfax stared at her and then slowly moved forward. "Elise, my dear, I have watched my son in the years since your engagement was broken and I know he suffered greatly for your loss. Now I look at him and I see...there is his spark again. His joy."

Stenfax shifted as Elise and his mother both looked at him. "Come now, Mama, don't make Elise think I was sitting in a pit of despair for three years."

Lady Stenfax blushed and said, "Perhaps not a pit, but I'm glad to see the light in your eyes again. If Elise has given that to you through her return to your life, why would we care one whit what anyone says about it? If one person dares question your union, I shall give them a harsh set down myself."

Stenfax bent his head with a slight chuckle, inspiring a glare from his mother. "I'm sorry, Mama, I just have a hard time picturing you handing out set downs."

"You think it's not in my nature," she said. "You forget what a disciplinarian I was to you all when you were children."

Now Gray and Felicity were laughing as well, and their mother turned toward them with an arched brow.

"Come, Mama," Gray said, reaching out to take her arm. "Let's go into supper and you can tell Rosalinde all about how you punished us so harshly as children. I think Felicity and Stenfax and Elise will join us momentarily."

Stenfax sent his brother a briefly grateful look as Felicity's face fell. Once they were alone, she stepped toward Elise and Stenfax. "Something has happened?"

Stenfax shifted as he took his sister's hands. They were cold and shook in his, and his heart sank. How he hated doing this. How he hated all of it.

His face must have looked stricken, for Elise slipped a hand in to cover both his and Felicity's. She gave him a gentle look and then said, "Felicity, dearest, there has been a development. Stenfax, may I?"

He nodded slowly, staring in wonder as she drew his sister to the settee and quietly told her about the new Duke of Kirkford's murder and how the book had likely been found by his cousin.

"It is in code?" Felicity said at last, her face drawn and pale.

Stenfax moved forward, shooting Elise a look of gratitude that she had taken over this duty. "Yes. Gray and I already delivered it to one of John Dane's allies in the War Department. They are working on it and will make sure Dane has a copy, as well, when he joins us in Caraway Court."

Felicity bent her head. "Well, then we must just wait, mustn't we? Until we can regroup and consider our options, it seems we are in a bind."

"I'm sorry, Felicity," Stenfax whispered.

She looked at him, her brow wrinkled. "It isn't your fault,

Lucien. But I need a moment. Will you have Mama begin supper? I'll join everyone shortly."

She squeezed Elise's hand, then got up and slipped from the parlor. Once she was gone, Elise slowly rose and moved over to stand with Stenfax. "She took it as well as could be expected," she murmured.

He shook his head. "Thanks to you. If I had given her the news, I would have said too much. Or not enough. How did you know I needed your help?"

She turned slowly and lifted her gaze to his. "It was just a sense I had. I'm glad I was of assistance, Lucien. I know I've blown apart your life, and it will blow apart more once the scandal sheets get word of Kirkford's murder and our engagement. The least I can do is try to make myself useful. Perhaps if I do, then you won't end up utterly regretting this decision you've made to wed me."

He cupped her cheek, smoothing a thumb over silky skin. Her lips parted slightly at the action and her pupils dilated. Touching her inspired the same physical reaction in him. But it was more than that. Being with her did exactly as his mother had observed a few moments earlier.

It brought back joy he hadn't realized he lost. Anticipation for his future that had been torn away when she left him.

"I don't feel regret," he said, unwilling and almost unable to say more.

So he spoke with his body. He leaned in and kissed her, and she lifted up on her tiptoes to sink into his embrace. After a moment, he reluctantly pulled away.

"We probably shouldn't start something we can't finish," he murmured, sliding his lips across her cheek, letting his hand trail to the smooth skin on her upper arm.

She shivered. "Probably not," she agreed, even as she nuzzled the spot where his neck and shoulder met.

"Come on," he said, grabbing her hand. "Let's bring an end to this extremely long day."

She nodded as she let him take her to the dining room, but

as they joined the others and he made an excuse for Felicity, he had a stark realization. Although this had been a long day, he wasn't actually all that eager for it to end. For all the bad of it, for all the horror, it was also the day Elise had been returned to him.

Now he just had to figure out how to overcome all that had separated them. Not the years, but the real things that kept the wall up between them. Because he wanted a life with her.

He just had to figure out how.

CHAPTER TWENTY

It was almost another week until Elise found herself sitting in a carriage with Felicity and Stenfax, winding their way down the final miles to Caraway Court. She glanced down in her lap and scowled at what she saw there.

When she did so, Felicity let out a sigh and snatched the paper resting there. "Stop reading this tripe!"

She held it up, shaking the *Scandal Sheet* with one hand. It was a special paper, delivered once a week, that only detailed the scandals in Society. The paper that had been delivered the previous day, before the family left London, featured the murder of the Duke of Kirkford and a huge article about Elise and Lucien's engagement.

It was meant to be "blind", their names not used in the description of their scandalous past and reunion, but since the author had linked it to strongly to the murder, which was not blind, there was no doubt to whom the paper referred.

Not that London had been silent on the subject even before the article. Word of their engagement had gotten out almost immediately, and Elise had been receiving nearly constant calls from the curious and the judgmental for days.

She was exhausted, both mentally and physically. And it wasn't just the strain of the rumors that did it. Stenfax had been increasingly withdrawn in their remaining time in London. Oh, he had spoken to her, yes. But always in the company of others. And since that last searing kiss at his mother's home, he hadn't touched her except to escort her from one room to another.

Sometimes she caught him *watching* her…rather like he was watching her at the moment from his place across from her in the carriage. She felt like he was trying to decide something and she rather feared what that something was.

"How can I ignore it when the *Scandal Sheet* is the most popular paper in London that no one admits to reading?"

"Felicity is right," Stenfax said, taking the sheet and balling it up before he opened the carriage window and tossed it out. "Whatever is being said changes *nothing* of our plans. We'll be in Caraway Court a while for the wedding and then working on whatever plans we make for dealing with Roger. By the time we return, much of the gossip will have faded."

Elise wasn't so certain of that, but at present she was more troubled by Lucien's withdrawn demeanor than the tales being told. Why did he pull away? And how could she ever bring him back after everything that had happened?

The carriage slowed as they turned up the final winding drive to the estate. Elise looked out as the big house rose up in her view, as beautiful as she remembered it all those years ago. She had once loved it here and now all that love rushed back, and tears leapt into her eyes at the joy of returning when she'd never thought it possible.

"Here come Celia and John Dane," Felicity said, reaching out to wave.

Elise straightened, trying to see the famous Celia Dane. The woman who had once almost been the Countess of Stenfax. As the vehicle slowed, it turned, and she caught nothing more than a glimpse of dark hair.

She pursed her lips as the carriage stopped and the footmen rushed to free them. They helped Felicity down first and she heard her friend say Celia's name. Lucien went next and he turned back to help her down himself.

She smiled at him and he returned a rather distracted expression of his own before he drew her forward. Gray and Rosalinde were pulling up behind in their carriage, which also included Stenfax's mother, but he didn't wait as he faced Elise to the couple on the drive.

Elise stared. She'd seen this woman before, but only from a distance. Up close, there was no denying how beautiful Celia Dane was. She had coloring similar to her sister, dark hair with bright blue eyes and porcelain skin. She had a more mischievous look to her, though, a sparkle and a light.

Elise swallowed hard in the face of it. No wonder Stenfax had chosen her.

"Mr. and Mrs. Dane, may I present the Duchess of Kirkford," Stenfax said. "Soon to be the Countess of Stenfax."

Somehow Elise found her voice and extended her hand first to John Dane. "Elise," she said, her words faint. "The rest is too complicated and with the help you are offering us, I don't think it right to stand on such ceremony."

Dane took her hand and shook it. She'd hardly noticed him in her focused attention on Celia, but he was a handsome man with longish dark blond hair and a neatly trimmed beard.

"My lady," he said.

When he released her, she turned to Celia. The other woman was smiling faintly, but there was an expression on her face that let Elise know she was being watched, analyzed.

"Elise," Celia said at last, putting out her hand. "I've heard so much about you."

Elise balked and her hand fell away from the other woman's. Celia's expression softened. "Oh, I meant from Rosalinde. She has written me a few times since you and Stenfax renewed your engagement."

There was a true kindness to Celia's voice that put Elise at ease despite the utterly awkward situation. She nodded. "Of—of course."

At that moment, Rosalinde rushed up to the group, and she and Celia exchanged a fierce hug before she lifted up on her toes to buss Dane's cheek. "You look wonderful," Rosalinde said. "The beard really does suit you."

That elicited a quick smile from John Dane that entirely changed his serious face. But Elise's attention was drawn away as there were other introductions to be made and everyone buzzed politely for a while as Elise stepped back. She felt a little out of place here, with this group of people who knew each other so well. Funny since once she'd been in the inner circle.

"Mama," Felicity said when the chatter had faded a bit. "Rosalinde said you were tired on the way in. Why don't you go up to your room and have a lay in? I'll make sure you're woken before supper."

Lady Stenfax arched a brow at her daughter. "Trying to get rid of me, are you?"

Felicity laughed. "Indeed not!"

Lady Stenfax didn't look completely certain, but she shrugged. "I *am* tired—I do hate to travel. You all have fun chatting about whatever you all talk about when your old mother isn't around."

They moved into the house where Lady Stenfax and her maid left them for the family quarters. Once she was gone, Stenfax's smile fell and he faced the rest. "We'll have some privacy in my offices. Gray, will you take everyone there?"

Gray did so as Stenfax stayed to speak to his servants. Elise followed the others slowly, allowing herself to look around as she went past familiar portraits and furniture.

Suddenly Stenfax was at her side. "Are you well, Elise?" he asked, startling her with his presence and his question.

"I am. Why?"

"You are not with the group," he said, motioning to the others, who were now entering a room at the end of the hall.

She glanced at him. She had promised herself days ago that if she wished to earn his trust, to show him hers, she would be honest with him in every way she could. Now she shook her head.

"I feel silly saying it, but when I was a girl, I thought of this house as a friend. When I knew my parents were bringing me here, I was always excited. And yes, it was because I was thrilled at the idea of seeing Felicity and Gray and Asher...and you. But it was also because I felt so at home here. When I believed I'd never return, it was heartbreaking."

He tilted his head. "You are reacquainting yourself with Caraway Court?" he asked.

She nodded. "I suppose I am."

He took her arm, and the touch of him against her was enough to make her knees weak. He smiled at her. "Well, you'll have plenty of time to get to know the place again. After all, you will be mistress over it soon enough."

She caught her breath at the idea. Every time she was reminded of it, it took her off guard. It seemed she'd never get quite accustomed to this new reality.

They entered the office, and Stenfax released her and pushed the door partly shut. "My servants are bringing refreshments momentarily," he explained, all the softness gone from his voice. "So we won't be able to truly talk about this matter until they've left us alone. I trust your travels were not too hard, Dane, Celia?"

Dane shook his head. "Not too difficult, no. And Gray, the matter with the canal port was resolved."

Felicity stepped up to Elise to whisper, "Once Celia married him, Gray made Dane as a partner in his businesses."

Elise nodded. She'd heard plenty about Gray's success over the years. Kirkford had complained mightily about it when he was deep in his cups. She, on the other hand, had been pleased for him. He was a hard worker and deserved success.

"I'm surprised he didn't partner with Stenfax," she said softly.

"He tried," Felicity said with a sigh. "Especially since our brother has fought so hard to rebuild the family coffers after the excesses of past generations. But when Gray first took his small inheritance and began to build his empire, Stenfax saw it as too great a risk."

"Gaming was never his style."

"He feared it, in a way. Later, when Gray was making money, he asked Stenfax again, but Lucien was stubborn. He felt it was charity from our brother."

Elise's lips parted. "So he refused?"

Felicity sighed. "He was determined to do things his own way, almost as penance for what our father and grandfathers gambled away. As I said, stubborn."

The servants came into the room with food and drinks and Felicity moved forward to greet the housekeeper warmly. Elise watched as Stenfax did the same. His stubbornness was what she feared, after all. That he would deny them both a chance at happiness because he refused to trust her.

She could only hope she'd find some way to climb those walls. If not, her future would be dashed.

Stenfax closed the door behind his servants and faced the room with a great sigh. Everyone looked as pensive and on edge as he felt, but his gaze didn't seek comfort from any of them except one.

Elise.

She was who he looked for in the group. She was who he took some level of strength in. Perhaps that made him a fool. He didn't know. Right now wasn't the time to analyze it.

"All right, now we can really talk," Stenfax said with a motion toward Dane. "What have you discovered?"

Dane stepped forward. "My contacts in the War Department are troubled by the diary page you gave them. The code is...complicated."

Felicity wrung her hands. "Does that mean it cannot be broken?"

"All codes can be broken," Dane said, almost apologetically. "It's easier if one has a key, and certainly there must have been one at some point. Still, my former superiors wonder if this book of yours contains more than just nasty secrets the old Duke of Kirkford held over the heads of his peers."

Gray wrinkled his brow. "They think it's related to something bigger?"

"It could be," Dane said. "So they've given me permission to investigate the case in an official capacity."

Rosalinde gasped and her gaze moved to Celia. Stenfax followed it, but found his former fiancée looked calm in the face of this news.

"Celia, is that…" Rosalinde began.

Celia nodded. "Of course I approve. John may be retired from that life, but in this instance, I think his investigative mind is just what we need. And to protect this family, *our* family, we'll do anything."

Stenfax heard Elise suck in a quiet breath through her teeth, and when he looked, he found her staring at Celia, her expression unreadable. He wished it weren't. He found himself wondering what she thought of the young woman he'd once planned to marry.

"What about this cousin who committed the murder?" Dane asked. "What do we know about him?"

The attention of the room swung to Elise, and she swallowed, as if the intensity of it was troublesome. Slowly she shook her head. "You must understand that my husband's entire family are a rotten lot, with the exception of Marina's branch. They were raised with a great deal of entitlement, so when they've felt slighted in the past, they lash out. The situation with Lucien was a perfect example. Toby was willing to marry me, which is a permanent solution, just to cut Lucien down."

Dane's focus remained on her, as if he were reading her as much as the situation. Stenfax wondered what he saw. "Would Roger have considered Ambrose getting the title to be a slight?"

"Indeed," Elise said immediately. "The fight they put up over the lineage was all out war. Roger felt that Ambrose was fraudulent in how he proved he was born first."

"And was he?" Celia asked.

Elise shook her head. "I kept myself out of most of it, but I would believe it. Ambrose was a bastard who would do anything to get what he…wanted."

She paled slightly and her fingers lifted to her eye. Stenfax flinched at the motion. Her bruise was nearly gone at last, but he could well imagine the emotional response to the violent attack against her would last a while.

Dane pulled a notebook from his jacket along with a stubby piece of charcoal pencil. "Let's start with your late husband. Why do you think he collected secrets like whatever is in this book of his?"

Her lips pinched, like thinking about the family was entirely unpleasant, but she did it nonetheless. "Toby liked hurting people. He liked having something over someone. Collecting the secrets, even writing them down, would have given him pleasure." She shivered. "I can well imagine he saw this book of his as a trophy of his misdeeds."

Dane was scribbling, but he was also shaking his head. "Still, he would have to be the source of the code," he murmured. "Would it have been something he learned or was taught? Something he shared?"

Elise blinked. "Are you asking me?"

Dane lifted his gaze with a brief smile. "It's an old habit to muse out loud on these details. My apologies. Now, what about Ambrose? What would he have done with the secrets, in your opinion?"

"Ambrose was more about proving his worth," Elise said after she pondered the answer. "From the moment he was given the title a few months ago to the last moment I saw him, he was very attached to, almost obsessed with the idea that he should be respected. I can speak more plainly about this motives to do with me…if it would help."

Dane leveled his gaze on her again. "Would it be too difficult to tell us what you know?"

Her cheeks flamed bright, and Stenfax strode over to her in three long steps and placed a hand on the small of her back. Her tension was clear in the way she held herself and he stroked her there gently in the hopes his presence would be of comfort.

She glanced up at him, almost in surprise, but then her expression softened. "It is difficult but I'll do it."

Stenfax shut his eyes. Here she was, surrounded by strangers and people who had despised her up until very recently, and yet she was willing to risk herself by telling them personal and embarrassing facts.

But was *he* so willing? Could he give of himself as freely as she was at present? Could he be so brave? When he asked himself those hard questions, standing next to Elise as she gathered herself, he found he didn't know.

But he'd better decide quickly.

CHAPTER TWENTY-ONE

Lucien's gentle hand on Elise's back was unexpected but so welcome. His fingers brushed there, warm through the silk fabric of her gown, connecting them physically so she could share his strength.

And she felt it, pulsing there, flowing through her in this difficult moment where she would have to lay out the humiliation of the months since Toby's death. But if it saved Felicity, if it spared Stenfax, it would be worth it.

She'd certainly done far worse in order to fulfill those goals of protecting them.

"Ambrose always...*wanted* me," she said at last, her heart throbbing so hard in her chest that it hurt. "He made that very clear in both words and deeds for the entire time I was wed to Toby."

She shivered as she thought of Ambrose cornering her in parlors, insisting on dancing with her. She thought of him whispering inappropriate things to her. Of him making sure he would connect physically with her, despite any protests she made.

When she'd dared mention it to Toby, he'd flown into a rage...at *her*, and implied she had enticed his cousin. She had kept her anxieties to herself after that.

Stenfax's fingers gently stroked on, bringing her back to the present, and he whispered, "It's all right."

She nodded slowly. He was right, of course. The past she was currently addressing no longer existed. "When my husband died, his cousin began hinting he would like to…" She turned her face and wished she could melt into the ground. "I'm sorry, this is difficult."

"Take your time," Dane said, his voice very gentle and deep. It was rather soothing, actually, and without a hint of judgment. It helped.

"Ambrose wanted me in his bed," she admitted. "I refused, of course, but over time he became more and more insistent that he would have what he wanted since the barrier of his cousin was gone. When he at last told me about the existence of the book, it was clear he wanted to find to use it to compel me to his will."

Felicity made a soft sound of pain. "I know how difficult it is to live in that kind of constant fear. I'm so sorry, Elise."

Elise gave her a gentle look, for she knew their two situations had not compared in the slightest. "It isn't your fault, dearest. I assure you, the only people I blame for this situation are Toby and Ambrose."

Dane was making notes again, just as he had done when they spoke of Toby's motives. "So two men with personal reasons to collect secrets. Still wonder about larger implications, but there it is. Now tell me what you know about Roger."

Elise cleared her throat. This was an easier topic. "I've been thinking about that since I was told he murdered Ambrose and took the book. I don't know him as well, but I do think he's less emotional than Toby or Ambrose were."

"How so?" Dane pressed.

She shrugged. "Just more…pragmatic, I suppose. He wasn't as quick to anger, the situation with the title aside. He took his time more when he responded to things. And even his motives were different when it came to the title."

"What do you mean, different?" Gray asked.

"I remember Toby making a big fuss over the fact that Roger came from a poor part of the family tree. He and Ambrose were horrible to him when it came to his place. The reason Roger wanted the title so badly after Toby died wasn't about respect or even power. He was about money. I could see him using anything he uncovered for blackmail to grow his coffers even larger than the funds available to him as duke."

Dane stopped writing and lifted his gaze. "I see." He turned without another word and paced to the fire where he seemed to be considering everything he heard. The room was quiet as he did so, everyone seeming to be poised on the edge of a cliff as they awaited his next statement.

Slowly he turned and looked at them. "Are you waiting for me?"

Celia laughed. "You *do* have an air about you, love, that says you're on the verge of something great."

Elise smiled at the easy way they interacted. She was still uncertain about Celia Dane, but there was no doubt the young woman adored her husband.

He ran a hand through his hair absently and said, "Oh, well, I may be, but it's going to take some thinking and some research to get there. If Roger truly is interested in blackmail, though, that may make our job easier. We can trace a money trail better than a wispy guide of vengeance or respect. Tracking money was never my strongest suit, but I can do it."

Elise let out a long sigh. This seemed to be a terrible nightmare that would never end. Dane couldn't just wave a wand and magically fix it. Not that she had expected it, but in that moment she realized she had secretly *hoped* it would be true.

Stenfax cleared his throat. "Dane, you have something to start with. As for tracking the money, I have some thoughts on how we can make that easier. But for now, I think we should all rest. It was a long two days of travel following a very tense time before. There is weight to this situation and I don't want anyone collapsing under it."

Rosalinde smiled gently at Elise, always the first to offer tacit or spoken support. "And there are the final preparations for a wedding to plan anyway. We all need to be well rested for that."

At that, Stenfax dropped his hand away from Elise's back.

She stiffened at the loss of his support and tried hard to keep her reaction from her face.

Stenfax said, "Yes, of course, the wedding, too. Why don't we all rest a while and regroup in a bit?"

Dane was looking at his notes. "Yes, I can start gathering this and..."

He roamed from the room absently and Celia laughed. "Well, he's off to solve a puzzle now. You know, I'm not very tired. Stenfax, perhaps we could speak as the others go up to lay down?"

Elise jerked her face toward his at that suggestion. She was shocked at how much jealousy rose up in her at the thought that Stenfax would be alone with a woman he once intended to marry.

That the same woman was now married and seemingly in love with her husband made no difference. Elise still wanted to rush forward and hurtle herself between Lucien and Celia.

Of course, she did no such foolish thing. She had some tiny bit of pride left, after all.

"Certainly," he said as the others gathered themselves to go up to their chambers. "I'd love a moment to catch up."

Elise set her jaw. There was no argument she could make against this plan that wouldn't make her look like a foolish ninny. So she forced herself to say, "I look forward to a bed, I admit."

Stenfax broke his gaze away from Celia and his eyes flashed with brief want as he looked at Elise. She tensed at the sight of it. They had barely touched for so long, her body ached for missing him. And judging by his look, it seemed he had his needs, too.

That gave her some small sense of triumph, and she clung to that as she followed the rest of the group from the room and left Stenfax alone with the woman he'd once intended to marry not so very long ago.

"So," Celia said as she settled into a chair by the fire and took the cup of tea Stenfax had prepared for her. "You have had a *very* busy summer since I left London two months ago."

Stenfax smiled despite himself and sat down across from her. "It has been quite a thing, yes."

"You are the king of the understatement," she said with a laugh.

He shrugged. "If there is more to say, I simply lack the eloquence to say it."

Celia set her cup aside and leaned forward, more serious now. "She's lovely," she offered. "Prettier close up than the few times I saw her at a distance."

Stenfax swallowed hard. "She is the most beautiful woman ever to grace this earth."

Celia smiled. "Rosalinde likes her, which of course is a great recommendation."

"Rosalinde is a good judge of character," he said, arching a brow. "Are you going to dance around whatever it is you truly want to say?"

She laughed. "Funny how we got to know each other better only *after* we decided not to marry."

Stenfax smiled once more. That was as true a statement as had ever been made. When he'd been engaged to Celia, he had felt absolutely nothing toward her. He'd welcomed that numb emptiness at the time and told himself he could live with it. That he would do his duty as so many men had done before and live very happily without anything more passionate or real in his future.

Now he was glad he hadn't sacrificed them both to the altar of that foolish mistake. If he had insisted they wed rather than release her, protect her, when she had admitted she wanted more, Celia never would have found her future with Dane. Stenfax knew very little about him, but it was evident Celia loved him

189

and he her.

And more to the point, Stenfax wouldn't have had a chance to ever be with Elise again. The very idea of that cut him to his bone.

"It's complicated, though, between you."

Stenfax lifted his gaze to her. "And you call *me* king of the understatement. You know about our past. After all that has gone on, you even know the bits I only just learned myself."

"You think John told me everything?" Celia asked.

He tilted his head. "The way he looks at you? Yes, I think he told you everything. I think he couldn't help himself, for you two are so connected."

Celia leaned back in her chair. "Well, of course he did. I suppose you must be angry with her."

Stenfax caught his breath. No one had put it in terms of anger before that moment—even he hadn't allowed himself to do so.

"Angry?" he said, his voice shaking a little. "She sacrificed herself for me and my family. She ensured that Felicity wasn't sent to the gallows. Am I *allowed* anger?"

"Of course you are," Celia said softly. "If anger is what you feel, then pretending it away does no good. You are certainly entitled to it, I think. She sacrificed herself, but I know you. You are not a man who likes someone else to arrange his destiny."

He clenched his jaw. And there it was. The truth he had been trying not to face, part of the truth that was keeping him from truly giving himself to Elise.

"I...*am* angry," he said, the words gaining more power when he said them out loud. "I loved her and I was not even given a chance to have a say in what she did. She didn't trust me enough to give me the opportunity to do what needed to be done for *my* family."

Celia's face was very still, and she nodded. "I can imagine that is frustrating."

"Once again, an understatement," Stenfax said as he pushed to his feet and strode across the room to the fireplace. He clenched a fist against the mantel and faced her.

"She lied to me. I *know* it was to protect me, to protect Felicity and I realize that the person who suffered most directly for that lie was her. But damn it, Celia, what can I do with that fact? How can I build a future with a person who cannot fully trust me? Who I cannot fully trust?"

Celia stood and there was a world of understanding on her face. "When John and I began courting, you recall he was pretending to be someone else."

Stenfax nodded. "Yes, of course. But isn't that different? He was doing that as a duty to his country, it wasn't of his own choice."

She moved toward him a long step. "Elise was willing to sacrifice herself to a life of torture with a man who used her as a weapon against someone who had slighted him. Do you really think she didn't do that out of *duty*? Do you really think she would have done it if she felt she had any *choice*?"

Stenfax's hand loosened slightly. He cleared his throat. "Then tell me, Celia, how did you overcome it when the truth came out about Dane? You obviously love him and he loves you. You married him despite his lies at the beginning. Now you are building a new life together. *How* did you manage to do all that?"

Celia reached out and covered his hands with hers gently. "I did it by recognizing that my love for him outweighed everything else. I did it by asking him to tell me everything I needed to know about his past, about his life, about what had led him to what he'd done. When he surrendered all the parts of himself, even the painful ones he had never shared with anyone else, I realized he was willing to put himself in my hands. That he gave me his faith and so I could be free to do the same in return. Now, perhaps that isn't as important to you, because you already know everything about Elise."

He frowned. He *did* know her motives, of course. He didn't even question them. But did he really know *everything* he'd wanted to hear from her? Had he *truly* opened all the doors that were locked between then?

"Stenfax, it is clear, just as it has always been clear, that you love her very much," Celia said. "And any woman who was willing to do what she did for you certainly loves you. I could see that the moment she stepped out of the carriage on your arm."

He shut his eyes briefly, for it was like Celia was ripping a protective scab from a long held wound. The words of love had been withheld despite all Lucien and Elise had been through.

"Will that be enough?" he asked. "This great love that couldn't sustain us in the past?"

Celia smiled at him, a gentle smile and a knowing one. But in this he supposed she *was* wiser. Considering what she and Dane had been through, he *knew* it.

"Oh yes. It will be more than enough, but only if you allow it to be so. You *must* find what it is that will make you let go of that past. Otherwise you will never be free. And that is just as unfair to Elise as it would have been for you and I to marry when we didn't care for each other."

He nodded slowly. "You have given me a great deal to think about, Celia."

"I'm sure I have. And luckily you have a few days left to do that thinking before you wed." She stifled a yawn. "And I think I will leave you to begin that thinking, as I am feeling the effects of travel." She leaned in to kiss him on the cheek. "You deserve to be happy, Stenfax. And so does she. Don't be so afraid of surrender that you throw away a wonderful future."

She patted his hand and then slipped from the room, leaving him to ponder her words. Leaving him to ponder everything he had lost.

And everything he had to gain if he could only overcome the walls between himself and Elise. Walls he had erected, himself.

CHAPTER TWENTY-TWO

In the days since her arrival at Lucien's country estate, Elise had experienced a great many things. She felt like she was home again after a long absence, and yet she also felt like a stranger who was out of place. She felt part of Lucien's family again, thanks to the kindness of Gray and Felicity and Lady Stenfax. But she also felt entirely alone and isolated because Lucien continued to withdraw.

With a sigh, she pushed through the terrace doors and walked out across the stone parapet. The summer sun was warm around her, but there was a bite of autumn underneath as she walked to the stone edge and set her hands down on the rough surface.

Being here was an odd thing. Even odder still was that less than an hour ago, she had been declared Lucien's wife.

His wife. That had been her dream for so long, and yet it felt like a hollow victory now thanks to the past that had destroyed their happiness. Their future.

The door behind her opened and she turned to watch Felicity step onto the terrace. Her friend had a wide smile as she said, "There you are, Lady Stenfax."

Elise flinched. That title didn't yet sound right, even though it had been the one she'd dreamed of holding since she was a girl and had fallen head over heels in love with her best friend's brother. A love that had only grown rather than shrunk with the years.

But how could she gleefully embrace her new name when

Lucien was inside and that wall between them that was still insurmountable?

She'd hoped coming here would change things between them, but it hadn't. Stenfax had busied himself with investigation alongside Gray and Dane, while she was wrapped up in wedding preparation. It was as if they were in different orbits now, passing each other, but never allowed to touch.

Felicity slipped an arm around her and squeezed. "It's going to be all right."

Elise sent her a side glance. Her friend was putting on a strong face but she knew Felicity's abject terror was just below the surface. Even as Gray, Stenfax and now John Dane worked together to protect her, Felicity seemed resigned that they might not succeed. That the truth might come out and destroy her.

"I know they'll defend you against anything that comes," Elise said as a comfort. "But as for me…well, I don't know if I believe it."

"Gray and Stenfax are certainly determined," Felicity said with a glance over her shoulder. "And Dane is very clever."

Elise followed her friend's stare and through the window she could see Celia and Dane talking to Stenfax. "You were right about Rosalinde's sister. I *like* Celia, even if she did lay claim to Stenfax once."

"No, she never did," Felicity said, her tone faraway. "Only you have ever done that."

Elise flinched at that assessment and slipped from her friend's embrace to walk back to the wall.

"You don't believe it to be true," Felicity said.

"I don't know anymore," Elise admitted.

"Well, ask Stenfax yourself, for here he comes," Felicity said.

Elise spun around to watch Lucien walk through the terrace doors toward her. She tensed as she awaited his arrival, awaited how he would treat her and if she could bear the barriers between them.

"Congratulations again, Lucien," Felicity said, moving

toward him. He embraced her just a little too tightly for the sentiment and Elise saw worry line his handsome face. He erased it before he pulled back and leaned down to whisper something to his sister.

Felicity nodded, tossed Elise a knowing smile and then went into the house. Elise's heart stuttered as Stenfax now strode toward her, his gaze focused firmly on her. When he reached her, he caught her hand and lifted it to his lips.

"Have I told you today just how lovely you look?"

Elise blushed. "Not in so many words, but when I rounded the corner into the parlor where we wed, your eyes got rather large. Though to be honest, I wasn't certain whether you liked what you saw or were considering making a run for it."

A rare smile broadened over his face. "I was not considering running, I assure you."

"No?" She drew a long breath. She didn't want these walls between them forever. And maybe, just maybe she could start to tear them down after all. She threaded her fingers through his. "I am surprised to hear you say you didn't consider escape."

"You think I wish to escape you?" he asked, his smile falling and his tone becoming serious.

"How can I not, Lucien? This marriage was thrust upon you, I know it was your honor that dictated you wed me rather than a real desire." He opened his mouth, but she moved forward. "Oh, please, let me finish."

"Go ahead."

"I appreciate the protection, please don't misunderstand. But there is so much we've left unsaid. So much between us from before, from now. I hate to start with so much in the balance."

She waited for him to respond, to deny what she said or to walk away like he had been doing throughout the time of their short engagement. Instead he nodded slowly.

"I agree, Elise," he whispered. "We *must* talk it out at last. Let's sneak away, just us, and do that."

Elise stared up at him. She couldn't read his expression and that frightened her, especially after the chaos of the past few weeks. "Won't the others notice our absence?"

"In such a small party, of course they will," he said, taking her hand. "But Felicity will explain. Now come, we have much to do if we are to resolve things between us at last."

She frowned at his turn of phrase. Resolve things between them at last. The idea was not very comforting. After all, he could have many plans for their future that weren't going to end happily for her. Many couples in Society lived separate lives.

"You tremble," he whispered.

She nodded. "I do."

His expression softened. "Come on."

He tugged her forward gently, toward the winding staircase that led from the terrace to the garden below. He took her on a side path that led back to the front of the estate and to her surprise, a phaeton was waiting there for them. He helped her up, said a few soft words to the groom who waited there for them, and then climbed up beside her.

They rode off together, not toward the main gate of the house, but farther into the estate, down pathways she had last traveled as a girl when she came here with her family. She might have enjoyed the trip through her memories if she wasn't so afraid of the outcome.

Stenfax, on the other hand, seemed entirely at ease. He even whistled as they rode on and on, through twisting lanes, past the manicured lawns and into the quiet, wooded depths of the estate.

After twenty minutes on the lane, he rounded a curve and a cottage rose up ahead of them. It was a beautiful place, faced with large, round river stone. Smoke curled up from the chimney, welcoming them there.

"Your father's old hunting lodge?" Elise said softly.

He cast a side glance toward her. "Yes. It's been closed up for years since I never have time for sport anymore. But I've had reopened and aired out for a new purpose."

Her heart sank, but she said nothing as he parked the vehicle and came around to help her down. She stared at his hand reaching toward her, then back at the house.

"You are frowning," he said softly. "You don't like it?"

She cleared her throat. "I-I'm sure it's lovely. But please just tell me, don't try to make it a pretty thing."

His brow wrinkled. "Tell you what?"

"Is this where you'll...put me? I know this marriage has caused a scandal and with everything between us, I can hardly expect that you wouldn't want to send me away to the country. I'm sure the cottage is very nice and I'll—"

He held up a hand to silence her. "You believe I've had the cottage reopened in order to banish you to the countryside and protect my hide?"

When he said it like that, she hesitated. "I don't know. It isn't like you, I know that. But things between us have changed so much since the truth came out." She bent her head.

"Take my hand," he said.

She lifted her eyes and found him reaching for her again. With a sigh, she did as he asked, rocked by the electricity between them as he helped her down. He said nothing as he drew her forward and opened the cottage door.

She caught her breath. There were flowers throughout the space, her favorite pink roses, bright yellow marigolds, even fragrant lavender. A fire burned brightly, with wine and two glasses set up beside the rug spread out there.

This was not a prison. It was a hideaway. She looked toward him. He took a long step forward and cupped her cheek.

"Faith, Elise. Have a little."

She shut her eyes as his thumb moved across her skin. Once more she hadn't trusted him, just as he had accused her of over and over. Once again she had proved that the wall between them was one she had earned.

She bit back a sob of disappointment and forced herself to look at him. "I'm sorry," she whispered.

He shook his head as he closed and locked the door behind them. "The groom will follow down in a bit and stable the horse. I just wanted a place for us. A place for privacy, since the main house is brimming with people and plans. I wanted to be able to talk to you." He moved forward again and crowded into her space. She welcomed it. "I wanted to be able to do more than talk to you."

She began to shake. Out of need, yes, but also out of something more powerful. Her love for him shook her and her realization that at last he wanted to hash things out with her. This was her chance, perhaps her *last* chance, to set things right after so much wrong.

"Which would you like to do first?" she whispered.

A half smile tilted his face, and then he bent his head and his lips moved over hers. At first he was gentle, just brushing his lips back and forth. She melted against him, clinging to his lapels with both hands as his lips parted and he devoured her with all the passion that had been held aside for the past two weeks.

She arched into him, feeling his hardness, feeling him shake with the power of his need. Feeling everything else drop away, if only for a moment.

At last, though, he withdrew, staring down at her with dilated pupils. "I think talking first would be best. Once we start the other, I don't intend to stop for a very long time and it will only confuse the issue."

She was both disappointed by his physical withdrawal and anticipating his emotional one. Perhaps that was what inspired her to burst out, "You've been holding back from me, Lucien and I know—"

He lifted a finger to her lips and pressed gently, silencing her. "Shhh. Let me speak a moment. Please."

She fought to find that trust he requested, required and remained silent.

He drew away and looked her up and down. "I have watched you in the past few days, so calmly facing everything difficulty, so beautifully handling all that has been thrown at you."

She swallowed. His voice was so…gentle. She hadn't heard that gentleness from him in years. It almost broke her, but she managed to stay composed. "I've done my best," she said.

He nodded. "I've thought every day about our conversations, as well as my conversations with others. About trust. About the future. And yes, you are correct when you say I've held back. I've been trying to figure out how to overcome our past and my feelings."

She flinched slightly, his words lashing at her no matter how gently they were put. "Your feelings," she repeated dully.

"Elise, if I want your honesty, then I must be equally honest with you. So allow me to begin. When you told me what you'd done to save my sister, to save *me*, I had two reactions. One was deep sorrow and gratitude at your sacrifice. The other was anger. I was angry at you for not allowing me to help. Angry at you for making a decision that should have been ours to make. Not yours, not mine. *Ours*."

"But I explained—"

"Oh, I know," he interrupted. "I know your reasons. I hear them and with a little bit of distance, I can even accept that you were right about how if I'd known the truth, I'd have gone off half-cocked and quite possibly made the entire situation worse."

She wrinkled her brow. "And yet you were still angry?" she asked.

He sighed. "Yes. Angry that you were put in that situation. Angry that you chose to handle it as you did. Perhaps what I was most angry at was what we lost. I raged against a past that never happened and a future that couldn't ever be."

She caught her breath. "No?"

"No, because we are both different people and a great deal has happened between us. But that doesn't mean that I don't want our future to be a very happy one. Together. Do you understand my feelings?"

"Yes," she whispered when she could speak. "And I'm so sorry, Lucien."

He cupped her cheeks. "My love, I don't ask for an apology. What I am doing is trusting you by giving you my pain. Trusting that you will protect the wound and help heal it now that you understand."

"I would move mountains to heal it," she whispered, awestruck by what he was saying and offering. "But does that mean you've forgiven me? That we can start over?"

He drew back. "Not exactly. You see, while thinking about my feelings, I also gave a great deal of thought to what I want. I keep telling you that I need your trust to move forward, but I never defined what that trust meant to me. It was unfair. But in talking to a good friend, I realized what it was I needed."

Her lips parted. "And what is that?"

"You and I have known each other almost our entire lives," he said with a soft smile. "I know you all the way up until the moment that you wrote that letter breaking me away from your life. And yes, I've reconnected with you since that happened. But I have no idea what has happened to you to shape you in that time. I have no idea of your suffering or even any small joys you took while you were in the prison of that marriage."

She caught her breath. "You want...you want..."

"What I want, Elise, what I need, is to know what you went through. To know what happened to make you the person you are today. The person I married and pledged to share my life with today. Would you tell me that? Would you trust me enough to open up those guarded parts of your past?"

CHAPTER TWENTY-THREE

Elise took a long step backward and a wild terror lit up in her eyes that Lucien had never seen before. She looked ready to bolt, but he knew if she did, they might never have a chance like this again. And he wanted that chance. He wanted to be free and to have her be free with him.

"Lucien, you don't want to hear that," she whispered. "And I don't want to say it."

He frowned, watching her lips tremble, feeling her pain pulse just beneath the surface. "I asked, didn't I?"

She turned her face, breaking the tenuous link between them. "For weeks, you haven't asked," she whispered. "And I've been glad of it. You know enough, don't you? You don't need all the ugly truth."

"It isn't out of a salacious need that I ask this of you now," he explained, not rushing her or speaking sharply. "Or out of some desire to hurt or punish you. I want to hear your missing part, your broken story, out of..."

He hesitated. He hadn't said this yet. He didn't want to use it against her or manipulate her with it. But it mattered.

"Out of what?" she asked, her voice shaking as much as her hands.

"Love, Elise."

She turned on him, her eyes wide, and she swallowed hard. "Don't tease me," she whispered. "Please don't."

"It isn't a tease," he reassured her. "I love you. And I need you to put your trust in that and in me. *Please.*"

"It's too much, Lucien," she said, and the pain in her voice stung like fire. She was on the edge of breaking down.

"I know it's too much," he said softly. "Let me take it. Let me help you carry it. Please. *Please*."

She shut her eyes, and he could see her gathering herself, preparing herself. He prayed that she would give in to him, to what they could be and have. He prayed she would be his again, in every way.

"Are you certain this is what you want? Even though you can't take it back once you hear it?"

He nodded. "It's what I need, Elise. It's what *we* need."

"I was never Kirkford's wife," she said, her voice barely carrying in the quiet room. "I was his puppet. His toy. He brought me out when he wanted to show off that he had won. When he didn't...well, I was put back on the shelf."

Lucien shuddered at those words. "It must have been horrible."

She shrugged. "I was happy enough for it, I suppose. When he left me alone, I didn't have to *endure* him."

She emphasized the word, and they both knew to what she referred. He stiffened and asked, "Did he hurt you?"

"No. It wasn't like Felicity," Elise rushed to say. "But he wasn't gentle with me, either. My needs were nothing to him, just as no one's needs meant anything to him. He took, he left, I prayed he'd find something else to do and celebrated when he did."

"He did often, so I hear," Lucien said through clenched teeth.

Color filled her cheeks. "Oh yes, his infidelity was widely known. He bragged about it even with me in the room. I remember once we were hosting a party and I was standing with him and one of his friends. The friend complimented me, said I looked pretty, I think. My husband snorted and said, 'You should see my mistress'."

"God," Lucien said, fighting the urge to pace away. He had asked for this pain, he had to take it. To bear it and witness it.

"I'm so sorry, Elise."

"It was lonely," she admitted, "but I found ways to harden myself to it. To accept it. I know people said I was cold, but I was cold to protect myself."

He nodded. When he first saw her, he'd thought she was unaffected by it all. He'd accused her, at least in his mind and likely by his actions, of having no heart. Now he understood why she had buried it so deep.

If he could excavate that heart even a fraction, he was proud of that fact. And he knew it would be his job to protect it.

"I think the worst part of it all," she continued, "was how I was seen after I threw you over. I would never be free, not just of him, but of all the hatred felt by those who once loved or even liked me. I would never be free of your hatred. That broke me more than anything he ever did."

"No," he said, moving toward her at last. "I do not hate you, Elise."

She smiled at that declaration, but he saw her hesitation still. He heard it when she sighed, "Oh, but what does it matter now? It doesn't change what I did to you. I still caused you pain."

He frowned. "That is not the first time you've said that. You told me the same thing when I asked why you didn't tell me the truth even after Kirkford was dead and you and I found each other again."

She nodded. "And I still feel it is true. You have married me to protect me, but do I deserve that? Do *you* deserve the censure and gossip that is already spreading through London like a wildfire? Once again you'll be hurt by my presence in your life."

He stared at her, truly understanding her perhaps for the first time in years. "Our trouble is not that you don't trust me or that I don't trust you, is it? Our trouble is that you don't believe you are worthy of a future."

She made a strangled sound and he saw the truth of his statement reflected on her face. She tried to turn away, but he caught her arm and held her in place gently, forcing her to hold his stare.

"I forgive you, Elise," he said slowly, succinctly. "But if won't matter if you don't forgive yourself."

Tears slid down her face and she stared up at him with all her pain hanging on her every movement and twitch. "How can I?"

"Just say it," he whispered. "Just say it for a start."

She bent her head, and the words came out as a sob. "I forgive myself."

She buckled and he caught her, holding her against his chest as she wept. He felt the pain pouring out of her, like poison from a wound. He had no doubt that she would have to revisit this action, probably for a long time to come.

But for the first time since he saw her in Vivien's parlor a few weeks before, he knew that everything between then would be well.

He pulled away and smiled down at her. "Now tell me one more thing, Elise."

She wiped at her tears. "What?"

"Do you love me?"

She leaned up, putting her face close to his, never breaking away from his stare. "I never stopped loving you in the three years we were apart. When my parents died, I was utterly alone. I knew I had no one left in my life who loved me. And then your note arrived."

He winced. When she had mentioned to his mother her appreciation for her note of condolence, he had hoped that meant she had forgotten his. "It was not well written," he said softly.

"It was short," she admitted.

"Curt," he whispered, thinking of how he had written and rewritten and rewritten that letter. Until his hand hurt.

"But it meant so much to me," she said. "Knowing how you hated me but were still willing to reach out in my saddest moment. I kept that damn note for months until Kirkford found it and destroyed it. But he couldn't destroy my memory of it."

"I wish I had been there for you."

She shook her head. "You were, in my heart. And when I heard you were to marry Celia, I thought I would shatter from the pain of it. Kirkford crowed and I died a little inside. But when I found out your engagement had ended, it was the only light in my darkness. I knew I couldn't have you, even though Kirkford was dead by then. I believed I'd never even see you again, but still…you were there and in the world and you were free. It was a selfish thing to want, but I did."

He reached for her, overwhelmed by these continued confessions, but also by her absolute faith that he would hear and protect her. And now he would.

"Listen to me. You have me, Elise. In a way, you always did." He stroked her cheek. "And I promise you, from this day forward, as long as I have breath in my body, you always will. *That* is my wedding vow to you, not the ones said up at the house. This. I will love you until my world ends. And I will love you in the next."

Her face crumpled a little and he realized his own cheeks were damp. He didn't care. He could give her those emotions, too, and for once he knew he could trust her with them.

"I love you," she murmured, wrapping her arms around his neck. "And I will never waste a moment of this second chance. I realize that it is a rare and special thing."

"Good," he said, lifting her against him, off the floor as he cupped her backside and began to carry her out of the main room and up the stairs into the master quarters. "Because I think we've wasted enough of them already. And it's time to truly make you my wife."

Elise couldn't believe how much she and Lucien had laughed as he helped her undress. It was like confession, trust, forgiveness, had burned away all the bad and left only hope and happiness. Now she lay on his bed, naked, watching as he stripped away the last remnants of his own clothing.

Her heart stuttered and her breath caught as she looked at him. He was all wiry strength and coiled muscle as he stalked toward her. And he was ready for her, too, as proven by the thick cock that curled proudly against his belly.

"I've been waiting for this since we agreed to wed," he murmured as he took a place next to her. He rolled onto his side facing her and placed a hand against her bare skin.

She shivered at the press of his rough flesh against her softness. "I've been waiting for this almost all my life," she murmured before she leaned in to kiss him deeply, passionately, with all the love she felt for him and all the hope she now dared to have.

He smiled against her lips, lifting his hands into her hair as he rolled onto his back and drew her over him. She pulled away, understanding his surrender as exactly what it was. He was showing her his trust in her now.

And she wasn't about to waste it or this moment when she had control over their lovemaking. She sat up on her knees and looked down the long length of his naked body. In that moment she knew exactly what she wanted to do. She leaned in, gently kissing and licking his neck, sliding her lips across his collarbone, his broad chest.

He caught his breath as she inched lower, swirling her tongue around one flat nipple with the same focus and pressure that he had with her nipples so many times.

"What are you doing?" he murmured, his voice low and rough.

She looked up the length of his body even as she pushed his legs open with one hand, creating a space for her to kneel in as she worked her mouth over his stomach.

"Exactly what you think I'm doing. Don't argue."

He said nothing more, just settled back, his hands folded behind his head as he watched her intently. She kept her gaze locked with his as she kissed his hip then slid her mouth over and smoothed her cheek against his cock.

He made a strangled noise and lifted against her slightly. She smiled, her heart swelling with love and the knowledge that she could move him just as he so often moved her.

Slowly she darted her tongue out and licked the length of his cock, starting at the base and sliding up to the tip in one long, languid stroke. He responded by cursing, and she laughed.

"Is that a message to stop or keep going?" she teased him.

His eyes narrowed. "Whatever you do, don't stop," he said, his voice almost impossibly rough.

She licked him again, swirling her tongue around his length over and over and over.

Slowly she pressed her mouth around him, lowering herself to take as much as she could before she withdrew. As he moaned, she paid attention, sliding over him harder and faster, then slower when he clenched his fists against the coverlet. She found that even though she was doing this only for him, even though he didn't touch her in any way, her body grew heavy, wet as she took him. She snaked one free hand between her legs and restlessly touched herself as she brought him closer and closer to the edge.

Finally he moaned deep and low, and then he caught her arms and dragged her up his body.

"This is not where I'm going to spend for the first time with my wife," he growled before he crushed his mouth down on hers, shifting their positions so that his bigger body half covered hers, holding her in place as he smoothed a hand down her body and joined her fingers between her legs.

"I would very much like to watch you touch yourself," he murmured as he kissed her neck. "We'll put it on the list of ways to pleasure you later."

He pushed her hand aside gently and covered her fully with his. His fingers parted her folds, sending electric pleasure through her body as he pressed a thumb to her clitoris and two fingers deep into her wet, clenching sheath.

She moaned his name, arching against his chest as pleasure

rolled through her body in a slow, building wave. He watched her, breath heavy, eyes hooded as he stroked and stroked until her back arched and she shuddered out a climax against his fingers.

He lifted them to his lips and licked away the slick evidence of her release before he moved into the space between her legs and positioned himself there.

"Look at me," he whispered.

She did so, locking gazes with him without hesitation. She saw everything she'd ever wanted in his stare, everything she'd given up hoping for, everything that would come in their future together. And it was like looking straight into heaven.

She cupped his cheeks, smiling up at him in pure joy.

"You are my wife," he said, sliding into her in one long stroke. "My love. My life."

She nodded. "And you are mine, at last. Forever."

He crushed his mouth to hers as he took her in heavy, hard strokes. Her clitoris, still sensitive from her previous orgasm, ground against his pelvis as he took her, and she let out a cry as pleasure mobbed her a second time. He groaned her name loudly against her neck as she milked him, and then he spent deep inside of her, grinding his hips against her body as they shuddered together.

He collapsed over her, whispering all his love to her as she smoothed her hands over his back and held him close to her. It felt like a heavenly eternity, but at last he lifted his head and smiled at her.

"Am I crushing you?" he asked.

She shook her head. "I like your weight. It lets me know this is real."

He leaned in and pressed a soft kiss to her lips. "It's real."

He rolled to his side, gathering her up against him in the safety of his arms. She snuggled against his chest, at peace for the first time in what felt like forever.

"How long can we stay here?" she asked at last.

He smoothed a hand over her hair. "Days," he promised.

"Food will be delivered, we'll be left alone otherwise."

She glanced up at him. "But—but what about Felicity?"

He arched a brow. "Not exactly what I expected my wife to say when I told her we get a few days of privacy after our wedding."

She laughed and slapped his chest playfully, but her mood sobered as she said, "I only meant, shouldn't we be helping?"

Lucien shook his head. "Right now I don't think there's anything we can do. Dane is doing his research and Gray will be there to assist. And I have a thought about someone else who could help, but it will take a few days at least for him to receive the message I sent and either come here or send one in return."

"So you're saying Felicity is as safe as she can be," Elise asked.

"For now." He smoothed the tangled locks away from her forehead and she shivered at his touch. "We are going to find a way to save her," he promised. "Together, this time."

She nodded as love swelled inside of her. "Yes, together," she whispered. "It turns out we are far stronger that way. I'll never forget that again."

He leaned in to kiss her, erasing all troubling thoughts from her mind, making her lose herself in pleasure once more. And in that moment, she realized that anything was possible, everything would work out and all she ever wanted was right here in her arms.

EPILOGUE

Ten Days Later

Lucien stepped into the parlor, a letter in hand, and took a moment to look around the room. There was an incredible sense of rightness in what he saw. Gray and Rosalinde sat together by the window, talking softly. Celia and Dane were nearby with Felicity, looking over papers spread out on the table before them.

And then there was Elise. She stood beside the fire stirring her tea, and when he entered the room, her face lit up with pure joy, pure pleasure, a pure welcome home.

Despite the troubling circumstances surrounding Felicity, Elise and Lucien had been enjoying a wonderful honeymoon period. He woke every morning to her beautiful face resting next to him on the pillows. She found ways throughout the day to touch him, to connect with him. And at night they surrendered to so many varied pleasures that his body thrummed just thinking about it.

But most important of all was that, slowly but steadily, they were rebuilding the trust and bond between them. Being broken had been the worst time of his life, but the break had led to healing stronger than ever. When he looked into his future, it seemed almost too bright to believe.

And it would be, if they could resolve the situation with Felicity.

"Good afternoon," he said.

Elise moved toward him and kissed him on the cheek before

she said, "Would you like tea, love?"

"Nothing, thank you. Where is Mama?"

"Upstairs," Gray said. "She complained of a slight headache."

"Probably better, as I do have some news."

He saw Felicity stiffen visibly before she straightened up from her place standing with Celia and moved toward him. "News about me?"

He nodded. "Yes. Dane, I know you said that you are not as accomplished in tracing money trails as you are in other aspects of investigation."

Dane shrugged almost apologetically. "Indeed, it was never my specialty."

"Well, I have reached out to someone who has quite a deal of experience in financial dealings and he was once very close to our family, so he can be trusted."

Felicity's lips parted and her eyes went wide as she took yet another step toward him. "Lucien, you didn't," she whispered.

He wrinkled his brow, confused by the horror in her voice. "Didn't reach out to Asher? Indeed, I did."

Felicity made a soft sound, her face crumpling ever so slightly, and then she bolted from the room. Stenfax stared as she left, and turned his attention to Elise.

She was pale, but she met his gaze with a slight shake of her head. Rosalinde got to her feet. "Let me go after her. I know this is incredibly difficult."

As she left, Dane said, "Who is Asher?"

Gray and Elise exchanged a look, and Gray said, "The son of an old servant of our father. He was about our age and was sometimes allowed to join us in our games. We all looked at him as a friend."

"At least I thought Felicity did," Stenfax mused softly, staring toward the door where she had fled.

"She...did," Elise said slowly. "It's a bit more complicated."

Stenfax turned on her, eyes wide at that comment, but

before he could ask more, Dane asked, "So the son of a servant could help us *how*, exactly?"

"Our family paid for his education," Stenfax clarified, still trying to determine what Elise could have meant by complicated when it came to Asher and Felicity. "He is a widely respected solicitor now and has managed the finances of many a titled gentleman. If anyone knows about money trails, it's him."

"I see. Well, if you feel he would be of help, I'd welcome his expertise."

"Good, because I've received word he'll be here within a few days. I haven't explained the situation to him beyond that Felicity is in a bit of trouble and we need his help. I thought it better to explain the particulars in person."

Dane nodded. "I agree. No need to create more evidence with letters explaining Felicity's situation. I look forward to meeting him."

As Gray, Dane and Celia began to talk to each other again, Elise stepped up next to Stenfax, slipping her hand into his. He tilted his head as he looked at her. "Do you want to tell me what Felicity's outburst was really about?"

She touched his face gently and smiled. "Were you really so blind that you never knew Felicity was in love with Asher all those years ago?"

"What?"

She nodded. "She'll likely kill me for telling you, but you should know that bringing him here is a hornet's nest waiting to be knocked from a tree."

He sighed. "Well, it's a hornet's nest that could save my sister, so I am not sorry I'm risking it. Thank you for telling me."

She leaned in and kissed him, and his mind emptied of its troubles in an instant. When she pulled back, she said, "No more secrets. It's what I promised, it's what I meant."

He held her gaze evenly. "And it's what I believe, my love. With all my heart. Just as I love you with all my heart."

"And I love you. And once we've saved Felicity, which I know we will, I intend on spending the rest of my life proving it."

He cupped her chin, not caring that everyone else in the room could see. "My love, you don't need to prove anything. Not ever again."

Then he leaned down and kissed her. And for that moment, all was right in his world.

Excerpt of Adored in Autumn

SEASONS BOOK 4

Asher Seyton swung down from his horse and looked up at the dark and shadowy house that rose up before him. It had been six years since he last crossed the threshold up those eight stone stairs. Six long and sometimes lonely years that were haunted by memory and longing he'd never been able to fully suppress.

Now he was back and he'd have to face those feelings again. Fully.

The door opened at the same time a servant came rushing down to take his horse. Asher blinked as the young man gave him a smart bow and murmured something about taking care of the animal. He'd held that same job once. He'd held many jobs on this estate while growing up here.

"Thank you," he said before he began to take those eight stairs two by two. At the top, he was greeted by a familiar face, that of Taylor, the same butler who had served here during his father's time as the last Earl of Stenfax's valet.

"Mr. Seyton," Taylor said with a wide and very welcoming smile. "My goodness, it is good to see you again."

"And you, Taylor. You haven't aged a day."

Taylor arched a brow and shook his head. "You flatter, sir."

Asher shifted at being called sir by a man who'd once boxed his ears. A man who had also taught him how to execute a formal bow just like the one the boy had performed toward him a few moments before.

"You are up late," Asher said, shaking off the strange feelings that mobbed him. "It is after midnight."

"Lord Stenfax received your message that you would be arriving tonight very late," Taylor explained as he stepped back and motioned Asher toward the foyer. "I volunteered to greet you."

Asher caught a breath as he entered the foyer. The house looked exactly the same as he remembered it. Beautiful, fine, but still welcoming. Rather like the family who had resided here for generations. A family that had allowed him to sometimes be part of it.

Until…

Well, there was no use thinking of that. Not when he was…*home*? It oddly felt like home to him.

"It was kind of you to do so," Asher said and noticed that Taylor had his hand out. "Er?"

"Your hat, sir? And your coat?" Taylor said.

Asher shifted as he removed those things. "I am accustomed to this, of course, but not from a man *I* once called sir," Asher said with a laugh. "Is there no way for us to go back to a less formal interaction?"

Taylor's face softened. "You've made good of yourself, Mr. Seyton. You should embrace all that comes with. In the end, there is no going back, only forward."

Asher swallowed. Yes, those were good words and ones for him to keep in mind as he made his way through the tricky maze he would surely find here. After all, he'd been called under mysterious circumstances. Stenfax hadn't been explicit in his explanation of why Asher was needed so desperately. He had only written:

Felicity is in some trouble.

After that, nothing else had mattered. It would have taken being drawn and quartered for Asher not to make it here as soon as he could manage.

"How is your father, Mr. Seyton?" Taylor asked, drawing Asher's attention back to the present.

He smiled. "Well, thank you for asking. His hands bother him a bit, but he very much likes the sea air and the countryside that retirement affords."

He kept his smile on his face and did not add that he sometimes felt his father was hiding out. He'd never really been the same after his second wife had died. A woman Asher had never met, thanks to circumstances he still didn't fully understand even after decades. And after the situation with Asher, his father had declared he was done with service and quit his duties here rather unexpectedly.

"That's wonderful," Taylor said. "When the family returns to London in the spring, perhaps I'll have to take a day and make a call on my old friend."

"He'd love it," Asher said with a wider smile. "He's only a day and a half away from here, you know. I intend to call on him whenever Stenfax releases me from this duty."

Taylor's face pinched a little and Asher stiffened. Whatever was happening with the family, it was clearly bad.

"Well, you must be exhausted after your long ride," Taylor said. "A room is ready for you."

"My old one," Asher said with a grin. He wondered if his initials were still carved on the wooden beam by the window.

Taylor's face twisted in something akin to horror. "Of course not, sir. You have a chamber prepared for you in the guest quarters. The Rose Room."

Asher's eyes went wide. He had never considered that he would be placed as a guest in the house he'd once served. And in the Rose Room, so named because it overlooked the gardens. It was the one of the best chambers in the guest side of the house.

"I see," he said slowly.

"Shall I show you up?" Taylor asked.

Asher shook his head. "No, I remember where it is. You go to bed, Taylor."

The butler seemed a bit uncomfortable with that idea but then nodded slowly. "Very well. The boy who took your horse will also bring your valise up and leave it by your door before he goes to bed. You'll find it there in the morning."

Asher nodded. "I remember that well. Good night."

"Good night, sir." Taylor gave one of his smart bows and left the foyer.

Asher stared around him once more, then sighed deeply. He was here so late, it seemed he would have once more sleepless night before he discovered the truth...before he faced Felicity again. He wasn't certain if that fact made him pleased or frustrated. Both, perhaps. He needed the time to prepare himself, but he also longed to see her.

He took a deep breath and then climbed up the stairs. He'd slid down this banister once as a child, following behind the current Earl of Stenfax. Oh, how his father had boxed his ears then. He'd reminded Asher he was allowed to pretend, but he wasn't one of *them*.

Of course he wasn't.

He turned reached the top of the stairs. Go left and he would find his way to the guest quarters and the Rose Room where he could rest his head. Go right and he'd slip toward the family doors. He still knew Felicity's by heart. How many days and nights had he passed by it and gotten a powerful thrill knowing she was just behind it? Wondering what she was doing or wearing. Or not wearing.

He would have moved to his room, but just as he allowed himself a quick peek down the hall, Felicity's door opened and she, herself, stepped outside.

Asher nearly pitched over backward down the steep staircase at the sight of her. Her blonde hair was down in long waves around her shoulders and back and she had a dressing gown tied tightly around her slender waist. Her feet were bare and she held a candle in her hand.

She turned toward him and her breath caught at the same moment their eyes met. Her expression brightened with a brief moment of pleasure and for a flash she looked just like the innocent, bright and happy girl he'd known and wanted all those years ago.

But then she swept that reaction away, her expression becoming guarded. And even from five feet away, even by candlelight and dim lamp light, he saw something that broke his heart.

He saw the hollow emptiness in her eyes. It was masked as

bored sophistication, but he saw the truth.

"Asher," she murmured as she took a long step toward him.

His body clenched at the sound of his given name formed almost in half-time from those full lips he'd only tasted one time. Lips he still dreamed about, fantasized about.

Even now, his body lurched with want. His hands shook with the desire to stride across the short distance between them and sweep her up against him, feel her mold into his body until there was no space, no breath, nothing but her and him and them.

But it wasn't six years ago and he understood life so much better now. What he wanted wasn't possible. His father had said as much then, now he knew the truth.

A woman like Felicity was out of his reach.

"Hello, my lady," he choked out, reverting to formality to protect him from desires.

It was all he could do, in the end.

Coming January 2017

Other Books by Jess Michaels

SEASONS

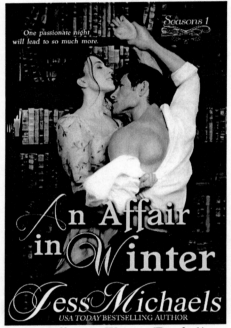

An Affair in Winter (Book 1)
A Spring Deception (Book 2)
One Summer of Surrender (Book 3)
Adored in Autumn (Book 4 – Coming January 2017)

THE WICKED WOODLEYS

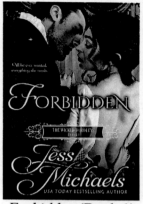

Forbidden (Book 1)
Deceived (Book 2)
Tempted (Book 3)
Ruined (Book 4)
Seduced (Book 5)

THE NOTORIOUS FLYNNS

The Other Duke (Book 1)
The Scoundrel's Lover (Book 2)
The Widow Wager (Book 3)
No Gentleman for Georgina (Book 4)
A Marquis for Mary (Book 5)

THE LADIES BOOK OF PLEASURES

A Matter of Sin
A Moment of Passion
A Measure of Deceit

THE PLEASURE WARS SERIES

Taken By the Duke
Pleasuring the Lady
Beauty and the Earl
Beautiful Distraction

About the Author

Jess Michaels writes erotic historical romance from her home in Tucson, AZ with her husband and one adorable kitty cat. She has written over 60 books, enjoys long walks in the desert and once wrestled a bear over a piece of pie. One of these things is a lie.

Jess loves to hear from fans! So please feel free to contact her in any of the following ways (or carrier pigeon):

www.AuthorJessMichaels.com

Email: Jess@AuthorJessMichaels.com
Twitter www.twitter.com/JessMichaelsbks
Facebook: www.facebook.com/JessMichaelsBks

Jess Michaels raffles a FREE Kindle or Amazon gift certificate EVERY month to members of her newsletter, so sign up on her website: http://www.authorjessmichaels.com/